The Thrice Named Man

Part II

Legionary

The Thrice Named Man

Part II

Legionary

by

Hector Miller

www.HectorMillerBooks.com

The Thrice Named Man
Part II
Legionary

All characters and events in this publication, other than those clearly in the public domain, are fictitious and any resemblance to real persons, living or dead, is purely coincidental.

Author: Hector Miller

Proofreading: Kira Miller, J van Rensburg

First edition, 2018, Hector Miller

Part II in the book series The Thrice Named Man

ISBN: 9781719874670

Text copyright © 2018 CJ Muller

All rights reserved.

No part of this publication may be reproduced, stored in a retrieval system, or transmitted, in any form or by any means, without the prior permission in writing of the author. Publications are exempt in the case of brief quotations in critical reviews or articles.

Contents

Chapter 1 – Recruit (October 235 AD) 1

Chapter 2 – Training 15

Chapter 3 – Weapons instructor 27

Chapter 4 – First campaign (January 236 AD) 38

Chapter 5 – March 46

Chapter 6 – First camp 53

Chapter 7 – Lussonium 57

Chapter 8 – Trap 68

Chapter 9 – Back on a horse 73

Chapter 10 – Battle 83

Chapter 11 – Aftermath 92

Chapter 12 – Centurion (September 236 AD) 102

Chapter 13 – Optio 112

Chapter 14 – Visit 120

Chapter 15 – Servant 130

Chapter 16 – The road east (February 237 AD) 137

Chapter 17 – Old friends 143

Contents (continued)

Chapter 18 – Thervingi 158

Chapter 19 – Kniva 171

Chapter 20 – Feast 179

Chapter 21 – Laws of hospitality 186

Chapter 22 – Holmgang (Trial by combat) 194

Chapter 23 - Spoils (July 237 AD) 205

Chapter 24 – Princess 207

Chapter 25 – Discontent 218

Chapter 26 – Meeting 228

Chapter 27 – Civilians (September 237 AD) 234

Chapter 28 – Aquileia (October 237 AD) 246

Chapter 29 – Rest 256

Chapter 30 – Master of weapons (February 238 AD) 266

Chapter 31 – Pannonian legions (March 238 AD) 273

Chapter 32 – The emperor arrives (April/May 238 AD) 285

Chapter 33 – Deliverance 293

Chapter 34 – Family heritage 301

Chapter 35 – Visitor 305

Chapter 1 – Recruit (October 235 AD)

"Name?" stated the clerk.

I hesitated for a moment because I had been called Eochar for years.

Before I could answer, the clerk looked up while tapping his stylus irritatingly on the side of the table. "Are you hard of hearing or just stupid? Name!"

I breathed deeply and replied: "I am Lucius Domitius Aurelianus."

While he wrote down my name he said: "State your trade."

Again I hesitated, but before he could intervene I replied: "Farmer."

He scowled and said: "That's not on the list, be more specific."

I could read well, even upside down, so I afforded a peek at his list.

"Huntsman", I replied.

He looked up from his writing, making eye contact and willing me to correct the obvious lie, but I kept quiet.

He mumbled "huntsman" while writing it down and continued: "Are you able to read and write?"

I decided to risk a question. "Would that be beneficial, sir?"

Again he eyed me with suspicion and replied: "Yes."

"I am able to read and write, sir", I said.

He wrote: "Claims to be literate, but it is highly unlikely."

The clerk pointed to an area where many new recruits congregated. "Wait there until you are summoned."

I strolled over to the group of at least six hundred recruits. These numbers were a good indication of the heavy losses taken by the Fourth Legion during the recent Alemanni wars.

All the young men were talking and laughing excitedly while standing together in small groups. Everyone knowing at least somebody. I hovered on the fringes, suddenly feeling lonely, and looked around for the opportunity to approach some or other individual in the same predicament.

I spotted another loner with eyes searching desperately, not unlike myself.

I approached my quarry in a wide arc. I stopped a pace behind him and said too loudly: "I'm Lucius!"

He didn't turn around, but kept his back to me. "Pleased to make your acquaintance, Lucius, my name is Vibius", he replied. "I hope you are better at fighting than at stalking people."

He had me on the back foot, but turned around with a broad smile on his face and clasped my forearm. "I really am pleased to meet you", he said. "It seems that everyone knows everyone, except you and me."

It was time for revenge and I replied: "Yes Vibius, I am."

He looked at me quizzically and I continued: "I am better at fighting than stalking." Both of us burst out laughing.

Vibius's father worked for the provincial administration somewhere in the east and had recently been transferred to Sirmium. He had not been in the area long enough to make friends.

I told him that my father bred horses nearby, but we had travelled extensively until recently, which explained my lack of friends.

Allow me to digress. I am inclined to speak the truth. Deceit is something I do not enjoy, but I could not share my past and experiences with my friends. Had I told them my truthful story, they would have ostracised me as a teller of tall tales.

I had lived with the Scythians of the Steppes, fought the brutal Goths and commanded seven thousand barbarian cavalry in a pitched battle. Even if they did, would they believe that I am a prince of the Roxolani and that I had been trained as a master of the sword by a priest from the land of Serica? I think not.

Would they believe that my father had murdered an emperor, or that the king of the Huns embraced me like a son? Never.

The only solution was to remain quiet about my past and keep my martial prowess hidden.

Before we could continue our conversation, centurions arrived and herded us into small groups.

We did not realise it then, but the centurions were the lead centurions of the ten cohorts of the legion. Each knew the number of recruits they had to gather to replace the losses of the recent campaign.

It is important to explain the position of centurion in a Roman legion.

The centurion commands a group of ten contubernia. A contubernium being a group of eight men who share a tent and live like a family for all practical purposes. He would normally have seen thirty summers or more, and possess sufficient practical experience in battle.

A centurion is not your friend. He represents the backbone of the legions of Rome. Practical, without mercy, but extremely capable.

Every legion is subdivided into ten cohorts and every cohort consists of six centuries. The cohorts are led by the centurion of the first century in the cohort.

The highest ranking centurion in the legion would be the centurion in charge of the first century of the first cohort. The Primus Pilus, or first spear, is only outranked by officers of noble birth.

Vibius and I ended up in the group of the centurion of the third cohort, Hostilius Proculus. In a certain way, he reminded me of Bradakos, my mentor during my sojourn in Scythia.

Hostilius was a brute. Heavily muscled, scarred and devoid of any visible compassion. Like Bradakos, he always carried a scowl on his face.

In any event, we ended up with Hostilius and that was that.

It was late in the day and we were shown to an area where legionaries had pitched tents for our use. The required tents were erected by each of the cohorts to accommodate their recruits.

The third had not suffered that heavily in comparison with the other cohorts and only four tents were erected to house the thirty-two new recruits.

Vibius and I shared the tent with six young men whose names I fail to recall. We curled up on our felt mats and I fell asleep almost immediately.

The night passed dreamlessly and I woke with a jolt when Centurion Hostilius kicked my leg.

"Wake up dogs, we are going for a little stroll around the countryside", he growled. "Get your arses outside and line up. Leave your belongings in the tent."

A few heartbeats later, thirty-two bedraggled young men stood in line, facing the officer. We wore a mismatch of clothes. Some had beards while others were clean-shaven. Hairstyles varied from close-cropped Roman style to Suebian topknots.

Hostilius allowed his eyes to slowly wash over us. I am sure I even picked up a hint of despair in his countenance as his scowl increased in severity, his knuckles visibly white as he strangled his vine cane.

He used his vine cane to point at the first individual in the line. "First recruit, one step forward, second recruit, one step back. Every second recruit follow!"

Chaos ensued. Eager to please, some stepped back while others stepped forward, leaving confused individuals in the centre, unable to fix the equation.

Hostilius's face matched the colour of his red cloak as he passed between the lines, yanking the recruits into the proper alignment by the scruff of the neck.

Next to the tents lay a heap of shields. They were all damaged in one way or another and probably used for training.

"Fall out, collect a shield, and fall in line exactly as you were", the centurion commanded.

The result was even worse than the first time. While everyone successfully gathered a shield, we were not able to identify where we fitted into the line. We ended up as a milling bunch, arguing about who was next to who.

The vine cane struck my back with such force, I was sure it had broken a bone. "You!" Hostilius yelled, pointing to a spot in the dirt with his cane. I complied.

As soon as he was satisfied that all were in position, he walked to the front of the column. "Follow me", he said as he marched towards the gate of the camp.

We did not march, we walked.

When we reached the gate, which was closed as per regulation, he yelled: "Stop."

Predictably, some of the men walked into the backs of others. Two even fell over.

Although the centurion knew exactly what the situation would be, he was kind enough not to turn around and mete out the required punishment. He just faced forward and waited patiently as the gates were opened.

I had trained with the curved oval roman shield, or scutum, as it was known by the legions and my left arm was used to its weight and feel. I normally trained with double weighted shields, so in comparison the one I carried felt light as a feather.

We had walked only five miles and I could see that most of the other recruits were battling with the weight of the shields. I emulated them, tried to look tired, and allowed my shield arm to sag.

The lengths we go to in order to be part of the collective!

Seven miles out of the camp the centurion called a halt. He had us turn to the side as if to enable him to discuss something with us.

I had trained with horses since before I could walk and I have been taught to scout by the Roxolani and the Huns, who are the best of the best.

I picked up on the approaching cavalry long before any of my fellow recruits noticed anything was amiss.

I was unsure what to do, so I extended my arm in front of my body, but I did not speak.

"What is your problem, soldier? Do you miss your mother?" Hostilius mocked.

"Small group of cavalry approaching from the north, sir", I said, and lowered my hand.

He raised his hand, signalling silence and turned his back on us, facing north. Within moments all of us could see the dust kicked up by approaching horsemen.

A group of thirty bore down on us at full gallop. They did not wear Roman uniforms, but were clothed in the style of the Scythians.

Hostilius yelled: "Barbarian cavalry approaching, brace for impact. Keep your shields locked and do not yield!" As he had no shield, he moved behind the shield wall for protection.

I knew what Scythian cavalry looked like. These horsemen were no Scythians. They rode badly, like Romans, and had Roman saddles and horses. Their clothes as well as their weapons and armour looked wrong.

Yet, facing a cavalry charge as infantry is one of the scariest experiences one can have. Then it dawned on me - it was a test.

The cavalry was a hundred paces away when I turned to Vibius and whispered: "These are not barbarians, my friend. The centurion only wants to see who will run. Relax."

At about forty paces out, three of the recruits could not bear it anymore. They dropped their shields and ran. The bogus barbarians reined in and halted ten paces from us.

My eye caught Hostilius watching the recruits intently.

He called to one of the horsemen and said: "Fetch back the boys who ran and bring them to me."

Hostilius stood a couple of paces away, awaiting the return of the cowardly recruits. Everyone was chatting excitedly and patting each other on the back. I focused and tried to listen to the conversation Hostilius was having. The three unfortunates were standing in front of him with eyes cast downward.

He spoke softly. "Not everyone is cut out to be a soldier. You three are not. You have not yet received the mark of the legionary and therefore you are free to go home. Do not be disheartened. If this exercise had not been done, your bloated corpses would soon lie on the field of battle."

He turned around, unaware of my eavesdropping, and yelled like only a Roman centurion can. "Quiet!" he boomed, his vine cane biting into the arms and legs of the recruits nearest to him.

"You may think that you are fortunate compared to those boys", he said, and pointed at the three walking down the road. "They are the lucky ones. You ladies now belong to me and I do not suffer fools like you. You will soon curse the day that you were born. Back to camp. On the trot."

I was the only one who did not vomit. I even had to fake looking tired when we arrived back at camp.

Trestle tables had been set out - one for each of the cohorts, attended by a myriad of clerks.

The twenty-nine of us lined up on the instruction of the centurion.

He stood next to the tables, observing the process.

Two wax tablets were laid out on the table.

"Gaius Cottius", yelled Hostilius. "Approach."

One of the young men stepped forward and came to stand next to the centurion.

"Can you read and write, Cottius?" Hostilius asked.

"Yes, Centurion", he replied.

"Read this" he said, "and then write it word for word on the second tablet."

Cottius smoothly read the inscription and proceeded to copy the text as instructed.

Hostilius handed the writing to a clerk who scrutinized it and nodded in acceptance.

"Congratulations Cottius", Hostilius said. "Welcome to the staff of the quartermaster. Your pay will be double that of a normal legionary."

He pointed with his vine cane to where Cottius should proceed.

"Lucius Domitius Aurelianus", Hostilius growled.

I saw what happened to Cottius and for the first time in my two-day long military career, I was paralyzed with fear on hearing the centurion call out my name.

If I were to end up in the service of the quartermaster, I would be a clerk for twenty years. I was horrified.

"You said that you are able to read and write. Is that correct or are you a liar, Lucius Domitius?" Hostilius said.

"I can read and write Centurion", I stammered.

A wax tablet was handed to me. The only thing I could come up with was to read the text, but read it badly, like a child would.

I looked up at Hostilius when I was done reading. His eyes narrowed and he pointed to the second wax tablet and stylus. I wrote, trying to draw the letters badly and change around the letters to confuse the reader.

The clerk checked my work and, scowling, shook his head. My gaze met Hostilius's eyes which were still narrow with suspicion.

He kept quiet and pointed to the spot I should move to. With relief I noticed that I was standing nowhere near Cottius.

When we had all performed the test, twenty-seven of us remained. A smiling Cottius and another recruit were escorted away to the section that would join the staff of the quartermaster.

It was late afternoon but I could see that the proceedings were long from being concluded.

We were again ordered to line up. We had to wait for a clerk, who arrived accompanied by four legionaries, carrying a heavy chest.

Each of us received our joining bonus of three hundred bronze sesterces. For me it was small change, but for some of the recruits it was more coin than they had ever held in their hands and they were visibly overawed.

I took the coin and tried to look pleased.

Once all of us had received the payment and made our mark to confirm the receipt, Hostilius took over.

"You will now take the legionary oath and receive the mark of the legion", the centurion stated.

We all had to face our new comrades and recite the oath, one by one: "I swear to do as my emperor commands, I swear to never desert my legion and I swear to give my life should it be required."

While we were giving our oaths, our names were entered into the rolls, as the oath would legally bind us to the service.

We then advanced to another table and one by one had the name "Legio IV Italica" tattooed onto the inside of our right wrists, just below the palm.

Once we were done, Hostilius clasped our forearms one at a time and said: "Welcome to the third cohort, legionary. Now you belong to me!"

Chapter 2 – Training

"Wake up ladies, time to look pretty for the party." The centurion's voice boomed around the tents.

In the early light of dawn the cohort barber had set up his mobile station and proceeded to cut our hair short and shave off our beards.

Barbering thirty men takes time. While we were waiting in line, the centurion shared some of his wisdom. "Let me give you some advice, boys. One day you will find yourself fighting for your life against some or other wild barbarian. Barbarians love their long hair and beards. Use it against them. Grab it and pull them closer so they can taste your iron."

"What do you see when you look at my face?" he asked no one in particular. Predictably he received no answer, so he raised his vine cane and pointed to Vibius, standing in line next to me.

Vibius was no fool and said: "Lots of battle scars, sir."

"Good, I see at least one of you has some sense", Hostilius said. "When you fight, your face tends to get damaged. The surgeon cannot stitch the pieces back together if you have a beard, boy."

About a watch later we were all clean-shaven, with close-cropped hair.

"Now that we've neatened you up, let's go get dressed up pretty. Follow me."

Hostilius escorted us to the stores of the quartermaster.

We were issued with the standard military clothing as well as hobnailed boots. We had to make our mark as proof of receipt. The value of the clothing would be deducted from our pay over a period of time.

We tried on the clothing to ensure that it fit properly.

It took forever for all of us to be appropriately attired, and we lined up for inspection before we left the stores of the quartermaster. Hostilius inspected us.

He stopped in front of a recruit: "Go get smaller boots, idiot. If you march in those, your feet will be bleeding before we leave camp."

He sent a couple more recruits back to exchange some or other garment, and once he was satisfied that all was in order, we marched back to our tents.

"Take down these tents", the centurion said. "You are now part of the elite third cohort. You will pitch your tents in the area set aside for my cohort, but you are still too stupid to be integrated with the veterans. We still need to sweat the stupidity out of you."

He left us to pitch our tents and prepare our evening meal. The veterans were housed in wooden barracks next to where we erected the tents.

The most basic skill a legionary must acquire is the military step. It does sound easy, doesn't it?

For one person it would be easy. To teach twenty-seven recruits to march at a certain pace and maintain formation is much more challenging, especially when most of them are dead on their feet from exhaustion.

We woke up early the next morning, as usual, and started the day with a five mile run.

Afterwards, we returned to the camp, prepared our own breakfasts and then we were back at training.

We marched for the rest of the day, practising our steps. Slow marching. Double step marching. All manners of marching.

We rested briefly during midday, and then it was back to marching again.

This went on for weeks, until we could run and march all day without anyone vomiting.

Centurion Hostilius Proculus did not attend to us every day. Due to his position as lead centurion of the cohort, he had to take care of other responsibilities, but he was the one who directed it all.

Once we could march properly, we were issued a set of lorica hamata, the chain mail armour of the legionaries, as well as a curved rectangular shield, known as a scutum.

We now trained to march in full armour, with shields. Again, it took time to master the little tricks of the trade. Hostilius showed us how to hold the shield in an overhand grip, and where to add extra padding to the undergarment to stop the mail from chafing.

But he was also relentless and brutal. Beating the stragglers mercilessly with his vine cane and meting out punishment for the merest infringement. I am sure that he would have blended in with the Huns. Those thoughts I wisely kept to myself.

All of the recruits were chomping at the bit to get proficient with weapons, but Hostilius refused.

"You will not touch a weapon until you can march perfectly."

Two months into our training we had managed to march the required twenty-four miles within five hours, without breaking ranks or falling out of step.

Although he tried to hide it, I could see our centurion was pleased. Not unlike the feeling you get when your favourite hound eventually manages to retrieve the waterfowl you had downed with your bow.

In any event, nobody tasted his vine cane that day, and on our return we went straight to the training field outside the camp. Fifty wooden posts were erected on one side of the field. The posts were a foot in diameter and stood the height of a man.

We all took wooden training swords from the racks next to the posts as ordered. The wooden swords were exact replicas of the legionary shortsword, or rather, the gladius as we called it.

These wooden training swords were twice as heavy as the real thing because it was weighted with lead.

"Choose a partner, ladies", the centurion said, and pointed to the posts.

We spread out so we all had our own post.

"Show me what you can do", the centurion said.

Some of the recruits attacked their post with vigour, slashing and stabbing like men gone mad. Others just stood in front of the posts and executed weak stabs and cuts. There were some who had obviously received basic instruction in the use of the sword and they stepped forward, performed a combination of three or four strokes and stepped back.

I cut at the post with sloppy slashes and for good measure I mixed in a few thrusts as well.

Hostilius called an end to the mess and said: "Lucius Domitius, with me."

I walked towards the centurion and he said: "I am going to attack you with slashes, try to defend."

"Yes, Centurion", I replied. He attacked immediately. I parried the strikes, trying to look clumsy.

We returned to our starting position and without warning he came at me with a perfectly executed thrust to the midriff. My countless hours of training caused my subconscious to take over and I stepped to the right, but at a slight angle, to ensure that the strike would miss my body. At the same time I allowed his blade to slide along mine. It would allow me to unbalance my opponent and control his blade while I moved in for the killing stroke.

My waking mind realised too late what I had done, but I tried to correct my mistake and I drew his sword onto my midriff. I took the hit on my armour, which was still very painful.

I could see Hostilius's eyes narrow but he willed back his comment and continued: "Do not waste your energy with wild slashing. That is the barbarian way. A well-aimed thrust is much more difficult to parry and will pierce armour, while a slash will not. A slash also opens up the attacker's body to counter-attacks, while a thrust does not. It is not necessary to bury your gladius in your opponent's body up to the hilt. Give him two inches of the tip, and he is out of the fight."

He proceeded to show us how a technically correct thrust to the midriff is performed. We spent the rest of the afternoon practising this move, with Hostilius making adjustments to our technique.

The centurion left early, with another centurion overseeing the afternoon's training.

We retired early that afternoon as a reward for our faultless marching.

Hostilius left instructions that we be allowed leave of the camp for half a watch to swim in the river.

We went as a group and arrived back at the camp clean and refreshed, albeit a bit tired.

I spent the evening preparing food and talking with my friend Vibius. We enjoyed the basic food and wine rations after the hard training of the day and went to bed early.

We rose before sunrise, prepared porridge, and reported for our morning run led by Centurion Hostilius.

That morning Hostilius was accompanied by another centurion.

"Centurion Tullius will join you on the run this morning", he said. "Lucius Domitius, you will stay behind."

I immediately sensed that something was wrong when I heard my name. The tone of his voice was different. It had a nervous edge to it.

The replacement centurion trotted off with the recruits in tow. I was left standing alone on the parade ground.

"Follow me", Hostilius growled.

We walked out of the camp and stopped next to the weapons training area where we had trained at the posts the previous day.

I was standing at attention and he said: "At ease, legionary."

He continued: "I decided to do a bit of investigation yesterday afternoon. I went to the office of the procurator and I ended up dealing with a filthy little Greek called Alexander. I enquired about a certain Lucius Domitius Aurelianus, to find out whether his father owns a farm in the area."

The scowl on the centurion's face intensified.

"Let me tell you what the Greek told me", he continued. "To be more specific, he didn't tell me anything, but he had some very good advice for me concerning my health. Do you know what he said?"

It was clear that I was in deep trouble. I just said: "No, Centurion."

"He told me that the road I am embarking on has just one outcome, and it ends up with my bloated corpse floating facedown in the Danube."

Hostilius took a deep breath to calm himself.

"He also asked me to leave his office and never show my face there again", the centurion added.

"I have been watching you from the start, Domitius", he growled. "You knew that men on horseback were approaching our group, and you sure as hell knew that it was a ruse. I watched you. You and Vibius were the only ones who didn't look like they were going to shit their breeks."

"I saw the effort you put in to sound stupid when your literacy was tested. Do you take me for a fool? You speak like the patricians do in Rome!"

I could see the anger rising in him, his jaw muscles clenching and unclenching and his face becoming blood red.

"Then you try and act like a novice at the posts. You may have fooled your fellow recruits, but I was not born yesterday."

"You run and you don't tire, and you look as hard as steel even though you are still a boy."

"I can see that even now your eyes hold no fear."

I had begun to breathe deeply, to calm myself and to be ready for any sudden move.

His hand went to the hilt of his sword. "I am going to ask you a few questions. Your truthful answers will determine both our destinies", he growled.

I nodded and continued to breathe.

"Beware, boy, do not lie to me. I have been a centurion long enough to smell lies a mile away."

"I give you permission to speak freely. Nothing you say will ever be shared with anyone else."

I nodded and said: "Thank you, Centurion."

He scowled and said: "Don't thank me too soon."

"Are you a spy for some or other faction of the Roman Senate?"

I looked him squarely in the eyes and said: "No, Centurion."

"Are you of the patrician class?"

"Yes, Centurion."

"Did you commit a crime and are you hiding from the law?"

"No, Centurion."

"Are you able to kill me at will in a sword fight?"

"Yes, Centurion."

He visibly relaxed but continued to stare into my eyes, as if trying to find some hidden deceit.

Hostilius walked to the racks containing the equipment and said: "Show me and don't hold back."

He tossed me a wooden gladius of normal weight and attacked.

Within a heartbeat he was lying on his face in the dust.

I extended my hand and helped him up. He accepted.

He walked back to the starting position and attacked me again, albeit using a different strategy.

The outcome was the same.

Hostilius was no fool with the sword, but I had studied under the masters of the sword for years and compared to me, he was a novice.

He eventually shook his head and said: "You truly are a master of the sword. I have never seen your equal. Not in the legions and not in Barbaricum."

"Who taught you?"

"I am honour bound not to answer that question, Centurion", I replied.

He frowned, the anger visibly rising at my rebuke, but then I saw him calm himself.

"Alright legionary, tell me then, why did you join the legions?"

"To serve the god of war, Centurion. It is what makes me content."

He did not answer immediately, but after a while he said, as if to himself: "I also am a servant of Mars."

"Where I come from, Centurion, we call him Arash."

Chapter 3 – Weapons instructor

I followed Hostilius back to camp. He was deep in thought, no doubt deliberating my future in the legion.

We were two hundred paces outside the gate when a group of Roman cavalry exited the camp and came trotting down the road.

We moved aside as they increased their pace and thundered past us.

I was preoccupied with my future and noticed little.

I heard the officer of the cavalry call a halt and the whole group reined in, but remained in their formation.

A young tribune came trotting up to us and dismounted, removing his magnificent plumed helmet.

Hostilius saluted the tribune and came to attention. Marcus walked over and embraced me.

"Well met, Lucius, I feel safer already seeing you here", he said.

He looked in Hostilius's direction, who, for the first time since I had met him, appeared utterly confused.

"Centurion, this man saved my life", Marcus added. "If you ever tire of him, send him to me. It will be your loss and my gain. He is the best horseman in the Empire."

"I would like to hear the story, Tribune", Hostilius replied.

"My apologies Centurion, but I am oath bound not to share it", he replied.

Marcus mounted and replaced his helmet, but before he rode off, he looked at Hostilius, who was still standing at attention.

"At ease, Centurion. Before I go, give me the name of the unit of this legionary", he commanded.

Hostilius relaxed and without pause replied: "He is the weapons trainer of the first century of the third cohort."

Marcus nodded, saluted, and thundered away on this horse, taking his place at the front of the waiting cavalry.

My centurion stared at me while shaking his head. "You never told me you were a horseman."

"You never asked, Centurion", I replied.

He scowled and kept walking. "Wait for me in my office", was all he said.

I was shown to Hostilius's quarters by a legionary, where his secretary told me to take a seat.

To exact some revenge he let me wait a full watch, or longer.

The centurion eventually showed himself and I rose, came to attention, and saluted.

He waved me through to his office. Lead centurions of cohorts were important men in the legion. They were well paid and enjoyed the services of a clerk as well as the necessary slaves and servants.

He sat down behind his rudimentary campaign desk and left me standing at attention, looking straight ahead.

"I have decided, as you have heard earlier, to appoint you to the first century of the cohort. You will also be the new weapons instructor, as your predecessor was claimed by an unfortunate arrow in the German campaign. It is unheard of to appoint a recruit as a weapons instructor. But the decision is mine and I have spoken", Hostilius said.

"I have more questions for you", he added. "Are you proficient with the use of the pilum and the bow?"

"Yes Centurion", I replied.

He scowled and said sarcastically: "How surprising. Which is your favoured weapon?"

"The bow, Centurion."

"With which other weapons are you familiar?" Hostilius asked.

"I have also trained with the heavy two-handed cavalry spear, the throwing spear, the long-hafted battle-axe and the lasso, Centurion. Mainly from horseback, though", I added as an afterthought.

Again he looked me in the eye, trying to find some deceit.

Eventually he looked away and said: "Good, collect your belongings and report to me."

Less than a quarter of a watch had passed when I followed Hostilius to meet the members of my new contubernium.

"Three of the legionaries of this contubernium died during our recent campaign", Hostilius explained. "When the recruits are fully trained, others may be added to bring it back to full strength."

I was on my way to become part of the first century of the cohort. Traditionally, the first century of a cohort contains the best fighters. Only the best veterans are advanced to this century, normally from the second century. These are the men who are in the front ranks, the ones who face the charge of the barbarians and survive to tell the tale.

It was late in the afternoon and the men had already retired to sit around their cooking fires. As we approached, the five men immediately jumped to attention and saluted.

"At ease", Hostilius said.

He pointed at me and said: "Meet your new tent mate, recruit Lucius Domitius. I suggest you be careful, he is a killer."

He shifted his gaze to me and said: "Report to me first thing in the morning, Domitius."

Hostilius abruptly turned around and walked away, leaving me with the five older men.

The eldest of the legionaries stood and clasped my arm: "Well met, youngster, I am the decanus of the tent party, but you may call me Felix." He smiled and continued: "Because you don't get close to retirement age if you are not one lucky bastard!"

Felix pointed at a small-framed man and said: "This is Pumilio, but do not be fooled by his size, eh."

I took Pumilio's arm and he clasped my forearm in a grip of iron, surprising for such a small man.

Next in line was a giant. He was as broad as he was tall. He had a generally mean and dirty look about him. As I approached he stood and smiled disarmingly. "Hello Lucius, I am Ursa. Pleased to make your acquaintance. Welcome to our family." I smiled back while he clasped my forearm with a paw reaching all the way around. He obviously tried not to hurt me and didn't squeeze too hard.

"This one is called Silentus", he said as a thin legionary of around thirty summers extended his hand to grip my forearm. Silentus nodded and sat down again.

"Don't mind him", Felix said. "He don't talk to us either, but he is useful in a fight". Silentus scowled and Felix winked at me.

"Last but not least, there is Bellus", Felix grinned.

In response, Bellus smiled a perfect smile, with perfect teeth, and clasped my forearm. "Well met, legionary Lucius Domitius. Do not be concerned, you will get a nickname soon." He pointed to a spot next to the fire and said: "Put down your pack and have a seat."

I sat down and Ursa poured me a beaker of cheap wine from a skin. He refilled the other beakers, raised his in the air and said: "To our new brother!"

I nearly choked on the terrible wine, but I managed to keep it down.

"Lucius, do not worry overmuch", Felix said. "All of us joined the legion for some or other obscure reason. Some of us talk about it", he gestured to Silentus, "and some of us prefer not to. None of us will ask. It is up to you whether you wish to share."

"Just remember that you are now our brother. Your survival depends on us as our survival depends on you. We share chores equally and fairly. It is not standard procedure to assign a new recruit to the first century. Actually, I have never seen it happen until today, but we trust Centurion Hostilius. He has saved our lives countless times, although he can be a mean bastard. If he says that you are a killer, I would rather have you on our side."

I told them that my father farmed horses in the vicinity of Sirmium and that we had travelled extensively over the past years. Whether I would share more, only time would tell.

Felix led me to an open bunk where I would sleep, and I placed my few belongings underneath.

I woke up early and volunteered to prepare some flatbread. I still had honey and olives in my pack and shared the last of it with my new family.

At sunrise I walked over to the quarters of the centurion to report as ordered.

I greeted the secretary who waved me through without looking up.

I stood to attention and saluted.

"We will start this morning with a short march of six miles", Hostilius said. "Next up will be weapons training. The men in this cohort are all veteran fighters. The sword champion of the cohort is obviously also in the first century. I want you to improve the skills of the first century to a level where they are the best in the legion. Can you do that?"

"Speak freely legionary!" he added.

"Centurion, there are some elements of fighting with the sword that I will be unable to teach. The grip I use took years to master and should I change their sword grip, they run the risk of dropping their swords in combat. Nonetheless, I believe that I could make them the best in the legion, although their technique will differ from mine", I replied.

"Good. I believe you", Hostilius said. "Would you be able to defeat two of the best swordsmen in the cohort simultaneously?"

"Yes, Centurion", I heard myself saying.

"Good. We need to prove your skills to the men. Dismissed", he said.

I saluted and joined the rest of my tent party.

Soon after the century marched from camp in full legionary armour with sword and pilum.

Afterwards we did not return to camp, but reported to the training area.

The century would usually consist of eighty legionaries, but due to the losses suffered during the recent campaign, only seventy one men came to attention in front of the posts, and on his command, faced the centurion.

"At ease, legionaries", Hostilius said.

The centurion was not one for long speeches. "We are the best century in the legion", he said proudly. "But", Hostilius added, "we can still improve. I want you to be the best by far. I have found a way to do that."

"Bassus, Fronto, go get two sparring swords of normal weight", he commanded.

I could feel the excitement as the men anticipated the duel between the two best fighters in the cohort.

Bassus and Fronto faced each other, but Hostilius held up his open palm to stop them. "Domitius, get one of the same and join them", he growled.

I had been breathing deeply for a while, to focus my mind and calm my nerves. I had an advantage over the two legionaries, as I knew what was about to happen.

Bassus was a big, muscular man while Fronto was small and lithe. It would not be easy, I thought as I approached the duo.

Hostilius turned to face my opponents. "You two will fight Domitius simultaneously, do not hold back", he said.

For a moment they were stunned, but then Fronto grinned. "Whatever you say, Centurion", he said.

They stood side by side, with Hostilius between us. Three paces separated me from the duo.

As Hostilius said "commence" I attacked immediately. I decided to take Fronto out first - he was the danger man, at least in my opinion.

I attacked from the right, placing Fronto between Bassus and me.

Although I preferred the thrust, I opened with a slash, from right to left, aimed at the stomach. Fronto parried. Just before our swords met, I altered the angle of the blade. His blade slid off mine, causing him to overextend his right arm. I moved in, pivoted on my left heel and hit him on the back of the helmet with the hilt of my sword. He collapsed, stunned.

Brassus attacked immediately when he saw what had happened to his friend.

He lunged towards me, aiming a mighty thrust at my chest. But his eyes gave away his intentions and I stepped back with my right foot, pivoted my hips and angled my body sideways, with my left side facing the attack. His wooden blade scraped along the rings of my mail. As he withdrew, I did not disengage as he expected, but moved in with his retreating sword, turning to face him, thrusting my sword with power and control into his stomach. As he doubled over, I hit him on the side of the head with the flat of the sword. He crumpled onto the sand.

It took only twenty heartbeats for me to defeat them. Even Hostilius's mouth was slightly ajar in amazement.

I walked over to Brassus and helped him get back on his feet, then I walked over to Fronto and did the same.

Hostilius faced the century and said: "Who has an objection to Domitius being the new weapons trainer of the first century?"

Silence.

"Permission to speak freely", he added.

Predictably, no one had an objection.

"Good. Domitius, you are now formally appointed as such. The clerk will enter it into the rolls", Hostilius commanded.

Chapter 4 – First campaign (January 236 AD)

When we had completed our training and other duties, we were dismissed to our quarters.

Felix was the first to comment on the happenings of the day. "You said you travelled with your father. Did you go to live with the war god? I had never seen anything like that, and I have been in the legions for twenty years."

"Yes Felix, something like that. I actually lived with people meaner than the war god", I replied.

"Boys, we are done fighting", Ursa said. "Next time we just send Lucius on ahead and loot the corpses when we reach the enemy!"

All the others, except Silentus, of course, had some wise words to add. I felt that I had proved my worth and I was one step closer to gaining acceptance from my new family.

In any event, we sat down next to our cooking fire and the conversation moved to politics, or rather, what passed for politics around a legionary fire.

My knowledge of politics had always surpassed my interest, but Nik was a patrician at heart and he kept me up to date.

Ursa drank deeply from his beaker of sour wine and said: "I heard that the Yazyges have allied with free Dacians to create an alliance against Rome. They are amassing on the banks of the Danube across from Pannonia Inferior somewhere south of Aquincum."

Felix was sharpening his gladius with a whetstone and replied without looking up: "Sure thing, Ursa, did the legate confide in you while you were enjoying a drink in his quarters?"

Ursa scowled, but continued unperturbed. "No Felix, my source is far more trustworthy. A messenger arrived from Aquincum today, bound for Singidinum and the IV Flavia Felix, where the emperor is staying for the winter. The messenger just changed horses, but he had enough time to enjoy a beaker of heated wine with the guard on duty, who is a distant cousin of mine. Obviously he swore my cousin to secrecy, but Nelius immediately spilled the beans. I'm sure the legate doesn't know yet, although he may be the only one in the legion who doesn't."

Pumilio raised his eyebrows and added: "At least we have a soldier emperor nowadays. The best news I had in a long time was when they told me that pretty boy Alexander Severus's throat had been cut. Good thing they took care of that bitch of a mother at the same time. I heard they got paid to do it. Should have come to me, 'cause I would have done it for free."

"Severus wanted to give our coin away to pay off the Germani barbarians. Cowardly bastard. Well, after they slit his throat, the Thracian took over and we paid them off in blood rather than gold. We chased them halfway across Germania and slaughtered the bastards real good, didn't we?"

"Maximinus Thrax is a man you can follow", Pumilio said. He took a swallow of wine. "Domitius, have you ever seen the new emperor in the flesh?" he asked.

I shook my head.

"He is a huge bloody bastard and strong as an ox", Pumilio continued. "Taller than anyone I've ever seen. He can speak Thracian fluently and he doesn't take shit."

"Pumilio, sounds like you are describing your mother", Bellus jested.

Pumilio scowled. "Stuff off pretty boy, you were the only one who liked Severus", Pumilio replied.

Felix interrupted them. "Shut your trap, Pumilio. The walls have ears. Remember, they will crucify the whole contubernium if they hear talk like that!"

Pumilio rolled his eyes and turned away to focus on getting the rust off his chain mail.

I ate well, drank more than enough bad wine and laughed a lot. In short, I enjoyed the evening.

We trained at weapons every day. I worked closely with Hostilius to improve the swordcraft of the century.

I had watched the men while they were sparring and identified the main area of weakness. Footwork.

Cai Lun, my teacher from the land of Serica, had made me perform countless repetitions of footwork combinations, simulating attack and defence. He had incorporated back and leg strengthening exercises into my routine. Most of the power of a sword strike comes from a combination of the back, hips and legs.

I was relentless. For ten days I focused only on this, training side by side with the legionaries, invariably until one or two had to be encouraged by Hostillius's vine cane.

We were preparing the evening meal when Ursa tried to get up to pour himself more wine. He couldn't. "Lucius, you truly are a mean bloody bastard. For the sake of the gods, I can't even walk. How will I fight if I can't bloody walk?"

By the third week I had them spar against each other and I showed them how to use their newly acquired strength.

I could see the realisation on some of their faces when they felt the power generated by the back and legs surge through their sword arms. Even Hostilius nodded in agreement.

Pumilio said to me: "I can't wait to test my new skills on our barbarian friends across the river."

He did not have to wait long. That same afternoon Hostilius came to us and said: "Start packing ladies, the emperor and the IV Flavia Felix are joining us in three days. Then we march to war."

The camp suddenly erupted into controlled chaos. Officers issued orders fast and thick and legionaries scrambled everywhere, carrying provisions, weapons or just messages.

We did not have much to pack, but I made sure my weapons and armour were in good condition. Felix gave me very good advice. "Lucius, I am going into Sirmium on an errand for Hostilius. I could get you some stuff that would make the campaign bearable. I need coin though, these things don't come cheap."

I trusted Felix and I handed him the pouch with the joining bonus I had received a few weeks earlier. He nodded, and then he was off.

That evening he sat next to me and placed a leather-wrapped package on the ground between us.

From the package he produced a thick woollen cloak, waterproofed with lanolin, two pairs of thick woollen socks, fur leg wrappings and a small bag of wool. The wool puzzled me but he said: "Just make sure you take it with you. I will show you later."

He also handed me back some of my coins. "I know how to bargain!" he said.

Hostilius did his rounds later that evening, and after allowing us to stand at ease he sat down.

"Assemble in full battle gear tomorrow morning on the parade ground", he said. "We will be addressed by the emperor." He looked at Felix and added: "Felix, make bloody sure that all these buggers are looking pretty, eh."

"Sure thing, Centurion, the boys will be all dressed up nicely, and looking pretty", Felix responded with a grin.

Hostilius nodded, got up, and left. When we were done polishing and cleaning all our gear, Felix inspected everything. He was thorough. He told me to put a bit more effort into the shine of my helmet and pointed out one or two other shortcomings with our kit.

Waking up before sunrise, we helped each other to get into our gear and again Felix inspected us and adjusted straps here and there. He even drew our swords one by one and inspected it.

We had just finished donning our garb when Hostilius arrived. We all stood to attention, allowing the centurion to inspect us. Satisfied, he slapped Felix on the back, nodded, and left.

Less than a watch had passed when the whole legion was lined up on the parade ground. Nothing stirred, no one talked.

We waited for a quarter of a watch for the emperor and his retinue to arrive.

A wooden podium had been erected earlier to provide the emperor with an elevated platform so that he could be seen by all the legionaries.

I must confess, I was surprised when he walked onto the stage. He was a head taller than the tallest of his bodyguards. He had a hard, scarred face with close-cropped grey hair and his eyes wandered over the legionaries, scrutinizing them critically. The emperor was dressed as a soldier. He wore a white tunic under a magnificent set of lorica segmentata with gilded shoulder sections, obviously especially made for him due to his abnormal size. Although it was bitterly cold, a purple woollen cloak hung loosely over his broad shoulders.

He was a soldier and no patrician and orator, so he bluntly said in a deep booming voice: "Men, the Empire is under attack from a barbarian alliance. The Legio IV Italica and Legio IV Flavia Felix will march to crush them under our heel. They have already attacked Pannonia Inferior so we march with haste."

All was quiet.

He had the heart of a soldier. He smiled and added: "There will be rewards for bravery, there will be slaves taken, and there will be loot for all. We leave tomorrow."

An almighty cheer resounded from the parade ground. Maximinus Thrax waited for the cheering to subside. He looked over the assembled legion with obvious pride, turned on his heel, and left with his retinue.

Chapter 5 – March

Long before sunrise, the first century of the third cohort was ready to march.

Each of us had a T-shaped wooden bar on which we arranged our heavy packs. We would be constructing temporary camps so we had to include a wicker basket and spade, as well as two wooden staves as our contribution towards the palisade. Our shields were protected by leather covers and carried on our backs. We all brought five days' rations of wheat, a small flask of olive oil, as well as a dish and a cup, and last but not least, two skins, one filled with water, the other with wine. As we were marching to war, we marched in full armour with all our weapons at hand.

Each contubernium had its own pack mule which carried the tent, spare weapons, a cooking pot, a grain stone for milling wheat, additional waterskins and a selection of tools and other essentials.

The emperor rode at the head of the army, surrounded by his bodyguards and officers. Our legion led the way with the IV Flavia Felix following close behind. We marched on the Roman road, avoiding the snowy mud on the sides of the road. As a result there was little dust, making it bearable for the men marching at the rear of the army.

We were heading more or less north towards Aquincum where the Legio II Adiutrix was stationed.

Even though we were fit and had marched almost every day while stationed at the camp, marching on campaign is different.

For one, the kit you carry along is always heavier. The extra cloak, the pair of warm socks, the little pot of honey, all add up. The bar of the yoke eats into your shoulder, through the chain mail and undergarment. Then the boots start rubbing you raw because they stretch and your feet move around. This is where Felix's experience came in handy. On the second morning of the march he told me to take out my bag of wool. He showed me how to stuff my boots with the wool to prevent my feet from being rubbed raw. He also tied the remaining wool around the shaft of the marching yoke. It sounds insignificant, but it made a huge difference to my morale.

We did not construct a marching camp for the first four days of the campaign. We were moving through Roman territory and the scouts have not had contact with the enemy. As a precaution, sentries were posted nonetheless.

We marched together as a tent group and century. As Hostilius was the first centurion of the cohort, he spent most of the march in the vicinity of the first century, but occasionally drifted down the line to ensure that all was well in the cohort.

Hostilius had just finished one of these inspections of the cohort, and he fell in at the head of our century once again. Then I noticed something untoward. I heard the faint whinny of a horse. I was trained by the Huns, and my senses were sharp as a result. I risked calling out and said: "Centurion, request permission to approach."

Hostilius immediately fell out of line and slowed down untill he was abreast of me. "Speak, Domitius."

"This better be good", he added.

"Sir, I noticed cavalry activity on the other side of that copse", and I pointed in the direction where I had heard the sound.

"Explain", he said.

"I heard the whinny of a horse, Centurion", I replied.

"Carry on marching, but take your shields off your backs and carry them in your hands", he commanded down the line. "And pass the message on to the whole of the third cohort."

The centurions did not carry a yoke, only arms and armour. Hostilius trotted up to a mounted tribune nearby. He saluted and had a quick conversation with the tribune, who immediately trotted in the direction of the senior officers of the legion.

Hostilius arrived back and fell in next to me, on the left hand side of the line. "Better not be your imagination legionary, I don't like looking like a fool."

He was still speaking when I felt the slight vibrations associated with a heavy cavalry charge. "Heavy cavalry approaching, sir."

He looked me in the eye and said: "Are you sure?"

"You will see them in ten heartbeats, sir."

Hostilius then did something that showed he had immense trust in my capabilities. Allow me to explain. A centurion, even a senior centurion, do not call a halt to the march of two legions, especially when the emperor is riding about two hundred paces away. Stopping the march for no reason at all could have serious consequences for him, including demotion to the ranks.

"Column, halt. Ground packs. Face right. Prepare to repel heavy cavalry", he yelled in his booming voice.

The main strength of the Roman legionary is obeying orders without thinking or questioning.

We were drilled to do this and within six heartbeats we had executed his orders perfectly. Just in time to see heavy cavalry of the Yazyges burst from the covering shrubs seventy paces away. They were armed and armoured in the normal way of heavy Scythian cavalry. The riders and horses were both armoured to the teeth with chain and scale, with the rider carrying a heavy two-handed spear fourteen feet long. This deadly spear is called a kontos.

The barbarian cavalry attacked all along our line. We were the only cohort that was fully prepared. The front rank kneeled and grounded their shields, their spears jutting out from between. The second rank placed their shields on top of the grounded scuta with their pila protruding in a similar fashion. The third cohort presented a solid wall of shield and pila all along the frontage.

No horse, not even heavy cavalry, will run into a solid wall, especially one with spears protruding from it. At thirty paces out, Hostilius yelled: "Third rank, release pilum." One hundred and fifty pila were launched at the seventy odd Scythians who were attacking the third cohort. Most of the pila just bounced off their nearly impenetrable armour, but at least three found the lower, unprotected leg of a horse, or some obscure opening in the armour, causing horse and rider to go down in a tumble of limbs. The Scythians attacking the third cohort wheeled away at the last moment and disappeared into the greenery from which they had emerged heartbeats before.

We witnessed the devastation all along the line where groups of Scythians had attacked. Legionaries lay prostrate, impaled by heavy spears. Some were dead, some seriously wounded.

Thanks to Hostilius's warning, the emperor's bodyguards were on high alert and managed to keep him out of harm's way.

The Scythian heavy cavalry vanished as quickly as they had appeared.

I lowered my shield and stood at ease. Felix asked me within earshot of Hostilius: "Why do you seem so relaxed, they could sally against us again. Be on your guard!"

"No Felix, they will not attack again. Their horses will be spent. They had waited for us in ambush for a long time and they charged a considerable distance."

Hostilius heard my conversation with Felix and yelled down the line: "Cohort at ease."

Everywhere legionaries grounded their shields and drank from their waterskins.

Our cohort had taken no casualties. I took my waterskin and drank deeply.

I could not help noticing the dead Scythian and crippled horse that lay ten paces from me. I extended my arm and said: "Permission to loot, Centurion?"

He eyed me warily and said: "Granted, but only you, and make it quick."

Felix held my shield and pilum and I stepped out of line. The Scythian wore heavy gold chains and a torque of gold around his neck. I reached out and took his undamaged bow from his saddlebag, as well as spare strings and two full quivers.

Hostilius looked at me intently and shook his head. "You truly are a strange one", he said.

He then strolled forward and removed the gold from the corpse.

Chapter 6 – First camp

The army was in no condition to continue marching and the order reached us that the emperor had made the decision to construct a camp as soon as possible.

Every legion had a corps of engineers who specialised in identifying suitable sites for the construction of a marching camp. Once the officers gave their blessing, the engineers marked out the camp with stakes and chalk. Only then did the legionaries move in to do the work.

Even when you are not tired from a fight and a long march, digging a ditch and building a rampart is brutal work. Our cohort was assigned to a section of the ditch and rampart. The emperor ordered the ditch to be five paces wide, rather than the standard three paces. We worked for at least four hours. We lined the top of the outer edge of the completed rampart with the wooden stakes we carried as part of our baggage. Due to our involvement in the construction we would be excused from sentry duty during the night.

Hostilius supervised the work and now and again laid into shirkers with his vine cane.

When we were done, the centurion walked over and passed me a bundle of clean clothing. "Go and clean yourself up in the stream, legionary, and wear this. Take off your armour and leave it with me. My body slave will take care of it. We have an audience with the emperor."

I washed in the stream and donned the clean clothing as ordered. Hostilius sent for me, and his body slave assisted me to strap on the shining armour.

We walked down the Via Principalis to the Praetorium, the tent of the emperor.

Hostilius announced us to the guards outside the tent and they ushered us into the presence of the great man.

The tent must have been specially made for him, was my first thought. Maximinus was a huge brute of a man. He was standing next to a map, deep in discussion with his commanding officers.

As we entered, Hostillius and I both came to attention.

The emperor walked in our direction and said: "At ease."

He waved his secretary over, who handed him two purses.

He walked over to Hostilius. "Centurion, this is a reward for saving my life", he said. I later learned that it contained the value of fifteen thousand denari, the equivalent of three years' pay. "I am a soldier, and soldiers want coin, not praise. Do you agree, Centurion?"

"I agree, Imperator", Hostilius said, maybe too loudly.

The Thracian clasped his arm. "I will give you praise anyway. Well done Centurion."

He abruptly turned to me and handed me a smaller purse, his intelligent eyes studying me intently. Then he surprised me by speaking in near fluent Scythian: "Who was the barbarian, your mother or father?"

"My mother", I replied in Scythian.

"From which tribe?" he asked.

"The Roxolani, lord", I replied.

He nodded. "They are a noble people, and don't be concerned, none of these educated men are able to understand a word of what we are saying."

He clasped my arm with his enormous hand and I could feel his godlike strength.

He kept holding my arm and continued in Scythian: "I will be keeping my eye on you. Thank you for doing your duty to your emperor, soldier."

He dismissed us with a wave of his hand.

Hostilius and I both saluted and left. We walked back to the tent and I could see him weighing the bag in his hand.

Hostilius finally asked: "What did he tell you?"

"He told me that you would ask me, but forbade me to ever tell anyone", I said.

Hostilius scowled and shook his head, slapped me on the back, and walked to his tent.

Chapter 7 – Lussonium

I unstrapped my armour and made myself comfortable next to the cooking fire.

The rest of the contubernium knew where I had been and all waited wide-eyed for me to share my experience.

I stared into the fire and stirred the coals, seemingly deep in thought.

Ursa couldn't contain his curiosity and said: "Are you going to share it with us or just sit there like a mute?" He seemed to realise what he had said and turned to Silentus: "Sorry, no offence."

I took out the purse which contained two hundred gold aurei.

I placed five gold coins on the ground in front of me. Most of these men would never even have handled a gold coin. I now had their undivided attention. They stared at the gold as if mesmerized.

Slowly, coin by coin, I stacked each heap until there were five heaps containing thirty gold coins each.

"The answer is yes", I said, looking up at Ursa, as I handed him his thirty gold aurei. "I will share it with you."

One by one, I handed each of my friends his share of the bounty.

They just sat there, speechless, clutching the coins. Thirty aurei represented two years' pay after deductions for equipment, and the funeral fund.

Ursa again spoke first: "So, what did he say?"

"He said that if I ever have any shit with my contubernium, he will come here in person and sort you out!"

It took a heartbeat or two for Ursa to digest the information, then he slapped me on the back and burst out laughing, followed by the rest of the contubernium. Even Silentus joined in.

We did not strike camp the next morning. Our centurion informed us that the Legio II Adiutrix would be joining us during the day. They had set out from Aquincum in the north at the same time that we had departed from Sirmium.

The barbarian incursion was more significant than originally anticipated.

Allow me to digress. Hostilius spoke about the invasion of the Scythians. Some referred to them as Sarmatians or even the tribes by name. The Romans tended to classify the barbarians based on where they lived, and not with reference to their tribal origins.

My views had always been different. The Germanic people tend to be sedentary most of the time. They cultivate the earth and own livestock. They move from place to place, but much less frequently than the nomadic tribes. They own horses, but do not spend most of their waking time in the saddle. They mainly fight on foot, using spears and swords.

The Scythians are nomads. People of the horse. They do not cultivate the earth, but move around with their mobile tents following huge herds of horses, cattle and sheep. They have a horse-warrior culture, fighting mounted with the bow or using heavy shock cavalry armed with spears. I will not elaborate about the difference between Scythians and Sarmatians. For practical reasons, assume they are more or less the same.

The Huns, which I know well, live far to the east. They are similar to Scythians, although they are hardier, less civilised, fiercer, and are influenced by the eastern culture.

The Goths, who are a Germanic people, migrated southwest into the lands of the Scythian tribes. They either wished to assimilate these tribes, or assert some or other form of hegemony over them. The free Dacians and the Yazyges, to name but a few, are examples. As you well know, I was there when they tried to subdue the Roxolani.

In any event, although the Romans viewed it as an alliance of Scythian tribes, I knew that it was the despicable, oath-breaking Goths that were pulling the strings. They needed the skills of the fast-moving Scythian cavalry to strike deep into Roman territory. The Goths had learned of the riches of the Empire and they desired to take it. They also knew that should they not keep migrating west, the terrible Hun hordes would eventually come into contact with them.

The Yazyges who attacked us cleverly killed the cavalry scouts prior to executing the ambush. At least one hundred and fifty legionaries would not fight again on this campaign, either due to death, or serious injury.

The legion we were waiting for arrived in the afternoon. We later heard that they were also ambushed by the barbarians in a very similar way, and had lost eighty legionaries.

The following morning we struck camp and filled the ditches. We were eager to avenge our fallen comrades and the three legions set off to hunt down the invading barbarians.

We were told that the barbarians had taken advantage of the freezing weather and had crossed the frozen Danube at Lussonium, an auxiliary fort with a civilian settlement bordering it. As most of the auxiliaries were currently redeployed on the Agri Decumates against the Germanic tribes, only four centuries manned the fort.

We were not informed of what had happened at Lussonium. Everyone had been killed. The auxiliaries, as well as the townspeople, including women and children. Even the dogs were not spared.

It was horrific to behold. The bodies had been lying outside for a couple of days, but due to the cold, decay had not set in yet.

We constructed a camp and on the orders of the emperor, immediately proceeded to bury the dead.

Our cohort was fortunate to be tasked with digging a mass grave in the frozen earth. I say fortunate, because some had to load the bodies onto wagons and drag them to their eternal destination once we had finished the digging. No one complained about the back-breaking work.

The invaders did not set Lussonium to the torch as was their way. The smoke would have been visible for miles and would have revealed their location to the legions.

To our great frustration, we were ordered to stay in camp the next morning. Hostilius arrived with the explanation. "The scouts determined that the barbarians had crossed back over the Danube. They raided farms and settlements, murdered, pillaged and ran away like the cowards they are."

My gaze drifted over his shoulder as he was updating his century. A thick column of black smoke appeared on the horizon.

I pointed and Hostilius spun around to have a look.

"Bastards", he hissed. "Bastards. That's due south of us. Alta Ripa is under attack, mark my words."

Alta Ripa was a Roman fort, garrisoned by auxiliaries from Africa. Mainly Berber cavalry and some light infantry.

We were not the only ones who noticed, and soon we heard the sound of cavalry leaving the fort.

Felix said: "The officers are sending out cavalry to scout. They suspect a trap."

Felix had hardly finished speaking when he was interrupted. "Look, its burnin' all over", Pumilio said, motioning with his head in the direction of a column of black smoke rising over the northern horizon.

A group of cavalry left the fort and headed north, bound for the fort at Annamatia.

Hostilius summoned me soon after, a heavy frown etched on his face.

"I have just returned from the office of the head tribune of the legion. He relayed a direct order from the emperor. The Thracian wants me and you to scout to the north of us. We are not to scout on horseback, but on foot."

He scowled and said: "Our leader seems to have taken a liking to you." He paused and added: "The emperor awards success, but do not be fooled. He does not suffer failures. We have been forced into a dangerous game and the stakes are high."

We left the camp as part of a team of sappers tasked to collect firewood. As soon as we found a suitable spot, the sappers began to chop down dead trees.

Hostilius and I dressed for the occasion. It was bitterly cold and we would not survive if we were not protected against the elements. On our legs we wore full length braccae made from goat pelts, with the fur on the inside. We pulled on thick woollen socks and leather legionary boots.

Although it was a scouting mission, I wore my own high quality lorica hamata over my felt undergarment. Over this I wore a long-sleeved, loose-fitting tunic that reached to my knees. It was made from sheepskin, with a layer of wool on the inside.

For camouflage and additional warmth, we each carried long, hooded cloaks made from the fur of marmots. I selected these cloaks as I knew them to be effective from my time living with the Huns.

Although it was not a military issue weapon, I persuaded Hostilius to let me take my looted Yazyges bow. I think that he wanted to see whether I could use it. In addition I carried only my gladius. Hostilius took his gladius as well as a pilum.

We carried five days' worth of dry rations, as a cooking fire was not ideal on a scouting mission.

It was early afternoon and we had at least a watch left to put some distance between us and the camp.

Hostilius pulled me in close and whispered: "I will lead. Keep the gap between us at twenty paces and do as I do. That way you will stay alive."

I nodded in obedience and did as I was told.

The Roxolani are excellent scouts. I hunted with them, and the best of them taught me the tricks of the trade. The Huns are better. It is difficult to explain why. They employ the same techniques and have much the same knowledge, but it is as if they are animals.

They use their sense of smell and hearing to a higher degree. They feel the vibrations of cavalry. Maybe they are just more in tune with their surroundings?

They are intensely aware of the normal sounds of their surroundings and alert to small changes.

We were walking on a path used by deer and wild boar when I noticed a minute change in the sounds of the forest. A strange bird added its call to the normal background twitter. It could have just been that I was not familiar with the area, but it was not dissimilar from my farm close to Sirmium, where I had honed my skills.

A slight breeze was blowing into my face and I sniffed the air as I was taught.

I moved off the path into the undergrowth when I picked up the unmistakeable smell of unwashed human. My bow was strung and hung over my shoulder. I had wisely spent my time around the cooking fire during the last days to file down some of the arrowheads to create armour-piercing needle point arrows. Instinctively I nocked a needle point arrow, holding three more in my draw hand.

I moved through the shrubby undergrowth silently, keeping pace with Hostilius who was still on the game path, oblivious to the danger.

The huge Goth burst from the undergrowth five paces behind Hostilius, drawing back his spear arm to impale the centurion at short range. He shouted some unintelligible words in Germanic. Something about a pig and blood.

I had been told many times never to waste precious arrows, but in this situation I had to be sure. The first needle point arrow entered the back of his skull, while the second pierced his heart. The big Goth's momentum drove him into the wide-eyed Hostilius who was caught halfway in the turn, and both went to ground. This probably saved the centurion's life. The

Gothic battle-axe had a long shaft, and the second attacker used both hands to accelerate the broad, razor-sharp, iron blade in a head-high horizontal arc. He intended to take Hostilius's head with a single blow, but the blade only cleft the air. As he stumbled forward, wrong-footed by the blow, I released three arrows. Two needle point arrows entered his chest and a broad-bladed hunting arrow sliced into the arteries in his neck.

My teachers would have been appalled at the wasteful use of arrows, but I knew they could be retrieved.

Both attackers had landed on top of Hostilius, who was still visibly shaken, although he tried to hide it.

I walked over to the corpses of the Goths and took their scalps, using the proven Hunnic method.

Hostilius was still just staring at me and the bloody scalps in my left hand.

"Don't be alarmed Centurion. I won't keep it. This is just to confuse them", I said casually, and retrieved my pack from the undergrowth.

He refrained from speaking for some time, but used a piece of the barbarian's clothing to wipe the blood and gore from his tunic.

He looked me in the eyes and said: "When the tribune relayed the orders of the emperor to me, he told me that he is sending you with me to keep me alive. I assumed that he was jesting."

It was a statement, but I recognized the question within and I said: "Centurion, I spent a long time with warriors who are more akin to animals than to civilised men. They have taught me their skills."

He nodded and said: "Lead the way, legionary."

"Follow fifty paces behind", I said. "When I hold up my hand, go to ground immediately."

Chapter 8 – Trap

By afternoon we were fortunate to stumble upon a rocky hill, densely populated with ancient oak trees. It was snowing so we decided to risk a fire. Against my better judgement I ventured from our campsite with my bow and was rewarded with four fat pheasants.

Hostilius had managed to get a fire going while I prepared the birds. I cut the necessary rigging from the branches of a massive oak tree that we used for shelter.

We had earlier scouted the area and there were no signs of the enemy.

The oak kept away most of the snow falling from above, while the incline, upwind of our position, protected us from the worst of the blizzard. It was still bitterly cold, but the shelter and the prospect of warm food made it bearable.

I positioned the birds next to the fire, and soon they were roasting in the searing heat.

"I do not recognise the barbarians who attacked us this morning. They look different from the Yazyges", Hostilius said.

I turned the pheasants and said: "I know them well enough. They were Goths. The Goths is a numerous people who encroach on the lands of the Scythians. They are being pushed west by nomads who live to the east of their lands. The only option for them is to encroach upon Rome. They are trying to subdue the Scythian tribes - the more they do this, the more they adopt the culture of the Scythians."

"The Goths are hungry for new lands and plunder", I added. "This is but the start. They are a scheming race of people, who would not blink an eye to deceive."

Hostilius grinned and said: "They sound very Roman to me."

"You are not wrong", I replied. "The simultaneous attack on the two forts is a plan. A deception."

We did not keep the fire going throughout the night, and took turns to sleep. The following morning we woke up early, broke our fast on the leftovers and continued our journey.

The fort at Annamatia was still miles away, so we moved as fast as caution allowed. We kept off the Roman roads in order to avoid detection, which forced us to struggle through densely forested areas. This, at least, kept us from the eyes of the enemy.

Our destination was still five miles distant when we exited a particularly dense area and stumbled upon the bodies.

Close to the Roman road we found the remains of what used to be twenty legionary cavalrymen.

Some bodies had wounds caused by heavy barbarian spears while others were riddled with arrows. All the weapons, clothing, horses and saddles were taken by the enemy. The Romans were surely led into a trap.

We had not the time or manpower to bury the bodies, but marked the spot in our minds so that they could be taken care of at a later stage.

It was too risky to approach the fort during daylight, but we had to find out whether it had been taken.

Hostilius and I could approach to within a mile using the vegetation as cover. We sat down and enjoyed the leftover pheasant with hard cheese and olives while we waited for darkness to descend.

As soon as it was dark enough we crept closer to the fort to investigate. Campfires were burning outside the gate and I could hear loud chatter in Scythian and Germanic. Although it was dark, the gates of the fort stood wide open. It had been overrun by the Gothic alliance.

I motioned to Hostilius to remain where he was. I slowly crept closer. The fort was still intact and I could see no evidence of fire damage. There were no sentries and I could sneak up close enough to be able to eavesdrop on the conversations around the fires.

I lay in hiding, listening for close to a watch. When I had heard enough I made my way back to the centurion.

I told him what I had overheard. "The barbarians had lit a huge fire in the vicinity of the fort to draw in our cavalry scouts. They were waiting for them in ambush and killed them with overwhelming numbers. It was an easy victory. They stripped the corpses of their gear and clothing and took the horses. The barbarians shaved their beards and donned the clothing of the Romans and conned their way into the fort. As soon as the gates were open, they poured into the fort and massacred the auxiliaries. Food, gear and weapons were looted. They sing the praises of their high lord, a Gothic war leader by the name of Argunt."

"Did they mention anything about their plans?" Hostilius asked.

"It seems that Argunt does not like to share his plans", I replied. "I believe they do not know, else they would have spoken about it. They were deep into their cups."

We slowly moved through the undergrowth until we were at least two miles from the fort. The night was bitterly cold without a fire, but our fur cloaks made it bearable.

From experience, I knew that I had to sleep with the cheese and dried meat inside my cloak. I had to share mine with Hostilius the next morning because his had frozen solid.

As soon as it was light enough to travel, we headed in the direction of our camp, making haste.

The remainder of our trip passed without incident and we arrived at the main camp late in the afternoon. We reported to the head tribune, who took us to the commander of the army to report in person. The emperor was firstly a soldier. He had enough experience to know that a direct report was worth more than one filtered by another officer.

We were ushered into the emperor's tent, and both of us came to attention and saluted.

"Speak, Centurion", he said.

Hostilius relayed the main points of the scouting mission.

The Thracian did not comment, but dismissed us with a wave of his hand. Just before we left the tent he called out to Hostillius: "Centurion, did he save your life?"

Hostilius turned around, inclined his head in respect and said: "Your prediction was correct, Lord Caesar, he did indeed."

Chapter 9 – Back on a horse

The emperor was a soldier. Soldiers are not inclined to sit around, they act.

He acted immediately and decisively. We marched the following morning at first light.

We crossed the frozen river at Lussonium, close to the temporary camp. It had stopped snowing and the sky was clear, although it was nearly as cold as in the land of the Huns. We marched at a reasonable pace and at midday the river was ten miles behind us. The emperor had taken only two legions, leaving behind the Legio II Adiutrix at our marching camp at Lussonium. They would patrol the countryside between Alta Ripa to the south and Annamatia to the north, ridding the Roman lands of any of the enemy who still found themselves on the south side of the Danube.

We were waiting for the engineers to stake out the perimeter of the camp when I was summoned by Hostilius. "Domitius!" was all he said, and I knew what it meant.

The emperor was busy with whatever emperors did, so Hostilius took us to the man who was second in charge of the legion, the Tribunus Laticlavius. Normally the position would be given to a young patrician as a first step towards political advancement. The Thracian had abruptly inserted his own man, a grizzled veteran of countless campaigns. The position had become vacant when the previous tribune left for Rome in a hurry following the assassination of Alexander Severus and his mother.

In any event, Cornelius Carbo was a man of much experience and few words. We came to attention and saluted.

"At ease", the Tribune growled.

His eyes drifted over me and he asked Hostilius: "Centurion, do you ride well?"

Hostilius was like a younger version of Carbo and he replied: "I ride, sir, but not well."

He kept his gaze on Hostilius and said to his Greek secretary. "Pericles, bring me the young equestrian cavalry tribune."

He walked to his desk studying some maps of the area, leaving us standing around awkwardly.

Pericles returned with a cavalryman in tow - none other than my friend Marcus.

Hostilius and I both saluted.

"Have you met Tribune Marcus Aurelius Claudius?" Carbo asked.

"Yes, Tribune", I replied.

"Good. You will draw the necessary supplies and equipment and leave tonight", Carbo said.

"Centurion, you are dismissed. Domitius, collect your gear and return here", Carbo added.

I collected my gear and my bow from the contubernium's dedicated pack mule. Hostilius had reluctantly agreed to transport our scouting gear on the animal.

A short while later I was waiting outside the tent for Marcus to appear. I could hear that he was still being briefed by the senior tribune, although I could not discern what they were saying.

He made his appearance and said: "Let's get you a horse, legionary. Follow me."

"This is an important mission for the emperor. He wants us to have good horses", he said as we walked towards the area where the personal horses of the emperor were kept.

I could obviously not use the emperor's own mount, but I selected a horse for endurance and camouflage. A magnificent gelding - light brown with a dark marking between the eyes. I entered into a brief discussion with the emperor's groomsman to confirm that I had made the right choice. When I was satisfied, he fetched the horse, and gave me a saddle on loan. I followed Marcus to where the cavalry's horses were kept.

When the darkness provided us with sufficient cover, we left camp, first travelling two miles in the direction from which we had come to confuse any enemy scouts who might be watching us.

The moon was hidden behind clouds; it was pitch black. We left the track and entered the forest where we found a suitable spot to spend the night.

We were unable to scout the area so we spoke little. Only a fool would risk being discovered by the enemy just for the sake of idle chatter. We ate dried venison and cheese. Marcus even produced a skin of half decent red wine.

As was the norm, we took turns to sleep. The night was mild, probably thanks to the cover provided by the forest. My cheese and bread slept with me inside the cloak, and after an adequate breakfast we left to do the emperor's bidding.

The countryside close to the Danube was heavily forested, but slowly gave way to patches of forest interspersed with grassland. It was winter and the trees were devoid of leaves, providing less cover than in summer.

We walked the horses in silence, with Marcus leading the way. A quarter of a watch had passed when we stopped in a small deserted ravine. As we had scouted the area prior to dismounting, we could converse in low tones for the first time.

"Are you as good at scouting as you are with a bow?" Marcus asked.

"Yes", I replied truthfully, and added "sir" for effect.

"Don't be ridiculous, Lucius", he said, and grinned. "You obviously have to call me sir when we are with the army, but if you ever call me sir again in private, I will arrange a flogging for you when we get back to camp." He punched my arm to emphasize the jest.

"My grandfather on my mother's side was a senator", he said. "My father is an equestrian. When I met your father, Nik, he reminded me of my grandfather. I am not blind. I can see that he is a noble and that you are at least of the equestrian class, like I am. Why did you not join the army as a cavalry officer? By the gods, man, if your seniors could see you ride a horse, you would be a decurion!"

"You have no shortage of coin either", he added. "Even if I am wrong regarding your lineage, you could surely buy yourself an officer's position?"

I decided to be truthful, which must have been my Roxolani heritage.

"Marcus, my friend, you are correct. My father is a noble, but my mother was a Scythian. My father does not wish to advertise his lineage. But even if things were different, I would still have joined the legions as a ranker. War is in my blood, Marcus. I desire to see war from the view of the common soldier. I wish to be in the thick of the fight. But more so, I follow the god of war and I will follow my destiny. If it is meant to be, there may come a time when I will join you in the cavalry. If not, I will spend my whole career as a legionary."

He smiled his infectious smile and said: "You have not even been in the army for six months and already you have become the emperor's favourite. I will bet my last sesterces that you will be promoted before the year is done."

"Lead on, legionary", he said. "Although I am a tribune, we both know who the better scout is."

The Huns know how to scout the sea of grass. It is critical to keep to the low-lying areas. Use the streams and ravines, and when exposed, move slowly and stay flat on the back of the horse. The Hun scouts even teach their horses to lie down flat when commanded. Our horses would not be that well trained.

We were watering our horses in a deep ravine when I heard the sound of men laughing. I immediately muzzled my horse with my hand and gestured to Marcus to do the same. Horses tend to nicker when they become aware of the presence of their own kind. Once I was satisfied that the horses were calm, I crept up the side of the ravine to investigate. Fifty paces yonder, two

Yazyges warriors were slowly riding their horses in the direction of the ravine.

I scrambled back down the slope. We had the clarity of mind to walk our horses in the small stream that meandered through the ravine and consequently we left no tracks. Marcus and I hastily doubled back the way we came and circled the ravine.

Nearby we found cover in the form of a hillock overgrown with dense shrubs.

"We could have easily killed those scouts, Marcus, but that would have alerted the enemy of our presence", I said.

"Yes Lucius, the emperor has a plan, but he needs us to scout the area without rousing suspicion. He realises that the Gothic alliance is trying to eliminate our cavalry and attack the legions when they are robbed of their eyes and ears. The Goths know that the legions use the cavalry as scouts. The emperor plans on using our cavalry as bait to lure the Goths into the grasp of the heavy infantry. Then the iron fist of the legions will smash them."

"We also need to identify the best spot for the legions to ambush the Goths, once we have located their camp", he added.

We decided that we would wait until dark. The presence of the enemy scouts indicated that their camp was nearby. We could ill afford to be seen, as it would spell disaster for our plans.

Late in the afternoon we spied the Yazyges scouts returning the way they came. They were still riding leisurely and conversing loudly, clearly unconcerned about the possible presence of Romans. We let them pass and followed them on foot. The mounted scouts outpaced us, but that was of no concern, as long as we could locate their camp.

It was dark when we crested yet another hill. We did not have to crawl over the hill because the darkness provided enough cover. Marcus was leading when he came to an abrupt stop. I nearly stumbled into him. Spread out in the valley below us, were thousands of campfires. We had located the enemy camp.

I had seen camps of the steppe nomad armies, and based on my knowledge, estimated the numbers of the enemy to be fifteen thousand warriors, but it was impossible to be certain. My guess was that half was Yazyges cavalry and the rest Gothic heavy infantry.

We could not afford the luxury to wait until first light to make a more accurate estimation. Marcus and I jogged to where we had left the horses and headed for the ravine which we visited earlier in the day. It was close to midnight and after a quick meal of cheese and stale bread, we took turns to sleep.

I had the last watch, and as soon as the night made way to the pre-dawn light, I woke Marcus. We rode, munching on hard cheese. We had passed a couple of suitable areas for an ambush site the previous day, and now we inspected them in more detail, discussing the benefits of each one.

We eventually decided on a narrow valley, two hundred paces across. The sides of the valley were accessible to infantry, but it was strewn with rocks and gravel, which made it nearly impossible for cavalry to breach.

We rode with caution for the next watch, but once we were miles away from the enemy, we picked up the pace and made it back to camp with half a watch of sunlight to spare.

I safely delivered the emperor's horse to the groomsman and Marcus went to make his report to Cornelius Carbo.

When the horse was in good hands, I immediately reported to Hostilius. His clerk ushered me in without delay.

I came to attention and saluted as I entered his office. "At ease, Domitius", he said.

I told him of the scouting mission, the proposed ambush and the location of the enemy camp.

He listened intently, turned around, and produced an amphora of red.

"Now go. Tomorrow will be bloody", was all he said as he handed me the wine.

Chapter 10 – Battle

My contubernium displayed more interest in the amphora of wine than my recent whereabouts. Little did I know that their lack of curiosity was not rooted in ignorance.

Ursa filled his beaker for the second time and smacked his lips as he swallowed the unwatered wine. "This is real good stuff. You must have done something right to get this from old stoneface."

He took another huge gulp and said: "Do you know by what name they call you in the legion?"

Now they had my attention. I did not even know that, apart from my century, anybody else in the legion knew of my existence.

Ursa refilled his cup and continued: "They call you 'Umbra', the ghost."

Felix noticed my surprise. "There are three things that keep a Roman legion going, Umbra. Gold, wine and gossip," he explained. "Anything you do is public knowledge. Tent flaps do not block out sounds, eh?"

Pumilio smiled and said: "Tell us about the scouting, else we have to hear the story from the emperor's scribe's second cousin on his mother's side, who is also the wife of Hostilius's secretary."

I grinned, already defeated. "We found the enemy camp", I said. "I estimate their numbers to be fifteen thousand. Probably half infantry, half cavalry. The emperor is planning to ambush their cavalry."

Bellus smiled his perfect smile and said: "I hate the bastards with the arrows. An arrow wound leaves a nasty scar."

Pumilio replied: "Then you'd better stand next to Ursa. He is too big a target to miss. His shield only covers half of his fat body."

"Sure, Pumilio, sure. Have you had time to requisition a smaller shield so you can see over the rim when you stand on your toes?"

Pumilio slapped Ursa on the back, who choked on the wine. "I will just stand on Bellus's ego. That'll be more than enough."

The banter continued till late that evening. It was a way to steady the nerves and to forge bonds of brotherhood, which was essential for survival.

Animals are able to sense the approach of a storm even when the skies are still clear and the sun is shining. In pretty much the same way a legion can sense the approach of a battle.

It starts with the officers who are more focused and to the point. Soon it filters through the ranks until even the pack mules are edgy.

That is how it was the following morning when we marched from camp. The legion bristled with pent-up nervous energy.

Although the rankers were not privy to the plans of the commanding officers, I knew more or less what was transpiring based on my scouting of the area.

The IV Flavia would block the advance of the Goths once the retreating cavalry had passed through their ranks. My legion, the IV Italica, would be the stopper in the amphora, to keep the enemy horsemen cooped up in the valley by blocking their retreat as soon as they have been lured into the trap.

The valley was narrower on the eastern side and fewer soldiers were needed to block it. Great was our disappointment when the third and fourth cohort were given their orders.

Hostilius explained that we would be the reserve, in case the barbarian infantry somehow managed to attack the rear of the legion.

The whole legion needed to stay concealed until the trap was sprung. We hid on a sparsely forested hill close to the entrance of the narrow valley.

We heard our cavalry thunder past in the adjacent valley. They were made up of the surviving legionary cavalry of three hundred, and a mixed group of auxiliaries of about seven hundred.

It seemed like an eternity before we heard the cavalry return, followed by an almighty thundering of hooves that made snow fall from the branches. Shortly afterwards we were given the order to advance. The legion deployed with haste across the valley entrance, leaving the third and fourth cohort on the slight slope overlooking the valley.

In my humble opinion, there are only two groups of warriors on earth who have elevated their skill in warfare to such a high level that it became akin to art.

The first is the arrow-storm of the Huns. Ahead of their time, rehearsed to perfection. Death in motion.

The second are the Roman legions. Disciplined, skilled and devoid of mercy. Deadly fighters encased in iron, who grind down their opponents relentlessly. Never giving up.

One of the few weaknesses of the legions is their vulnerability against mounted archers. This is only true when the lay of the land favours cavalry. The situation unfolding before us favoured the Romans.

From far off we could hear the sounds of battle and see clouds of arrows rising and falling. The only evidence of the presence of the legion was the buccina issuing orders for the cohorts to advance, which was a good sign.

Soon the first Scythians appeared on our side of the valley. They reigned in when they realised that their retreat was blocked. Once enough of the enemy had amassed, they rode at the Roman line, releasing thousands of arrows.

The legion was well prepared and received the missiles with their shields locked tightly. The rear ranks of the legion formed the testudo by raising their shields above their heads, presenting a roof of shields to the descending arrows.

Most of the shafts ended up embedded in the shields, but some found the inevitable gaps between shields. Dead or wounded Romans were efficiently dragged away or assisted to the back of the line where medical orderlies were waiting.

The Scythians were good at their craft, but their bows lacked the brutal power of the Hunnic weapon. The Hunnic counter-rotating circle gives rise to the storm of arrows, designed to breach a wall of shields. No army of this world can stand against it. But these were not the barbaric Huns. The Yazyges were softened by centuries of exposure to civilisation, their nomadic culture eroded by agriculture. And they died.

When the milling horsemen came close to the Romans, some legionaries left the line and grabbed the reins of horses, allowing their comrades to pull the barbarians from their saddles. The fight turned into a melee on foot, which favoured the heavily armoured Roman infantry.

As the legions battled with the horsemen, Hostilius noticed the approach of the Gothic infantry. They were marching to the aid of the Scythians. The Goths outnumbered the reserve by at least three to one.

At its narrowest point, the valley was three hundred and fifty paces wide, allowing Hostilius to deploy his men with both flanks protected by the rocky rises of the valley sides.

We stood three ranks deep. The Goths approached us at a slow jog, chanting some Germanic war song. They were huge, fierce-looking men with long, blonde hair protruding from beneath their helmets. Half of the warriors owned mail, and most were armed with spears. Some carried long-shafted battle-axes and the nobles among them brandished Germanic longswords. Most protected themselves with round wooden shields.

At forty paces out, we launched the first volley of pila. The majority struck shields, but some found flesh. It did little to halt the advancing barbarian horde. The second volley hit the Goths almost horizontally at a distance of ten paces. More went down, some discarded shields rendered useless by bent pila, but still the horde advanced.

Hostilius, as was expected of the commanding officer, stood behind the ranks, enabling him to direct the flow of the battle.

"Here they come, ladies", he roared. "Brace!"

Most of the men of the IV Italica were veterans who had fought the tribes of the Germani numerous times and lived to tell the tale. Never before had I fought in the Roman ranks, but, for years, Nik had trained me to fight in the way of the legionary. I was not, but I felt like a veteran of many battles.

As they impacted our shields, we retreated two steps – a move executed in perfect unison. The front rank of Goths felt their support slip away and they staggered forward, into our gladii, thrust at head height.

As most of their front rank disappeared under our feet, the shield wall took one powerful step forward, went down on one knee, and thrust upward into the groins and stomachs of the enemy.

I saw a veteran Goth with bare arms, criss-crossed with scars, step over the body of the man who fell to my blade. His spear came at my mouth with the speed of a striking viper. I moved my head marginally to the left and the blade scored a line on the cheek guard of my helmet. He overreached and I pushed his shaft upwards by lifting my shield. I stepped forward and skewered his right foot with my blade. As he withdrew, I stepped in and my blade entered his mouth. Meanwhile, on my left, a giant of a man had hooked his bearded battle-axe over the rim of Pumilio's shield and was trying to dislodge it from his grip. My blade struck his unprotected neck like lightning, severing the jugular. Pumilio stepped in next to me as I dispatched Ursa's opponent by hammering the hilt of my blade into his temple. Ursa stepped forward and suddenly the once thick line of the Goths was bending. My blood was up and I used the skills I had acquired over the years to dispatch one opponent after another. Parrying, stepping in close, lashing out with lightning fast strikes. My next opponent's eyes darted left and right and I smelled the fear as I readied myself and stepped forward for an easy kill. Before I moved, the Goth threw down his spear and ran. For a moment in time, even less than a heartbeat, the man behind him looked at me, an apparition soaked in blood and gore, mumbled something, and followed suit.

The next moment they all turned and fled.

I just stood there.

"Now look what you did, Umbra", Felix said. "You went and scared them."

"I stopped counting after you killed twenty", Ursa added. "Some of them pointed at you before they ran and said 'Teiwaz'. I wonder what it means."

"He was too busy killing the Goths to listen to their grunting", Hostilius replied from behind me. "Unlike the rest of you ladies", he added.

Hostilius slapped me on the back. I grinned, and retreated to the line.

I decided not to comment, but I knew the meaning of the word.

Teiwaz is the name the Goths give to their god of war.

Chapter 11 – Aftermath

One in four of the Yazyges warriors died. Three or four thousand abandoned their horses and fled the battlefield as soon as they realized all was lost. The emperor accepted the surrender of nearly two thousand of the horsemen, and arranged for them to be sold into slavery. War was a profitable business.

The most valuable commodity captured was the herd of five thousand Scythian horses. These horses were sought after on the markets throughout the Empire. Quality specimens would fetch at least two thousand denarii each, with some as high as ten thousand.

The legionaries would receive a portion of the profit from the sale of the slaves and horses. Though my priorities were different to the norm, I also participated in the looting. I found a magnificent Scythian bow, far superior to the one I had looted weeks earlier. To the frustration of Hostilius and the pack mule, I ended up with five quivers of the best arrows I could find.

That evening we feasted on horse meat. We still had half an amphora of Hostilius's wine left. The rest of my contubernium excused me from normal duties like baking bread, and roasting meat.

"You killed more of those bastards than the rest of us put together", Felix said. "Killing is hard work, son."

The emperor was pleased with our performance and all the rankers were issued with double rations of wine. If not for that, Ursa would have caused our cups to run dry.

Bellus tore into the meat, the juices running freely down his chin. "The Goths ran quickly. That was the last we will see of them for years, if not centuries. They are broken. Same goes for the Yazyges."

Felix listened and said: "Don't be too hasty, Bellus. Umbra knows the Goths from way back. What do you think, Umbra? Will they return, or have they run?"

I drank deeply from my cup. "Felix is correct, I have a history with the Goths", I confirmed. "They are different from the other barbarian tribes. For one, they are as numerous as the stars in the sky. They outnumber the Marcomanni and the fierce Quadi by thousands. But one thing that makes them most dangerous is their cunning. They are using their allies to test us, to learn. The small infantry force that attacked us was only to show their commitment to the cause. Where were the rest of their infantry? Let me tell you. The best of them returned to their lair, sending just a token force to their death. So yes, they will be back, and next time there will be more and they will fight differently, they will fight better. They will abide their time, wait patiently and strike swiftly when they sense weakness of any kind. Our only hope is that the Huns annihilate them before they breach our defences."

"Who are the Huns?" Ursa asked.

"The Huns are a people that live beyond the land of the Scythians. Half men, half demons. They make the Yazyges look like children playing at war", I answered.

Felix stirred the coals and turned the meat. "Well, at least we don't have to fight these people. Umbra, if you feel this way about these Huns, I hope that they never covet the riches of Rome."

Pumilio added: "No use worrying about barbarians who live so far away that no one except Umbra has ever heard of them. I say we focus on drinking as much wine and eating as much meat as we are able to. That is what makes sense to me."

Silentus nodded in agreement and swallowed down another piece of meat with the cheap legionary issue wine.

That night I hardly slept at all. All was well, I had been accepted by my contubernium, and I even had a nickname. I had survived the battle and had met the emperor. I attributed the difficulty sleeping to the excitement of the day before.

We filled the ditches in the morning, and by the second watch of the day we were marching for the Danube. Even if you wake up refreshed, marching soon cures it. If you wake up tired, like I had that day, you feel like dying after a watch on the march.

"What's the matter Umbra, got nobody to kill today?" Bellus jested.

I just scowled, like my friend Bradakos had taught me.

In later years I became more in tune. I realised that a restless night or a strange feeling should never be shrugged off. One should accept these as premonitions and treat it as such. The gods speak to us every day, but not in words. They talk to us from within ourselves, and woe to the man who ignores it.

I first noticed it because I was marching next to the pack mule. I had been taught by the horse people of the steppes to pick up signs from the animals. Horses, and mules, will hear and smell danger long before a man will.

In any event, I saw the tell-tale signs as the mule's ears pricked up. I ignored it. Maybe it was due to fatigue, maybe it was tension leaving my body after the battle. The reason is of no consequence.

We marched through an area covered with dense shrubs, and when it came, the attack was swift and brutal.

Allow me to digress. I have always harboured a deep-seated animosity towards the Goths. I tend to sell them short, unlike the Huns, Scythians and Romans. The people of the steppes are expert horse archers. The Roman infantry is without match. To be fair to them, the Goths are born with a spear in their hands. It is hard to imagine, but they cast a spear with the same level of power and accuracy as a Hun shoots his bow.

They stormed out of the undergrowth and cast their spears with incredible force. I was preoccupied with my own thoughts, and as I heard the noise, I looked up and saw a spear imbed itself in Bellus's neck. Blood spurted all over my face. I was disorientated for a moment, dropped my pack, and stumbled to the ground.

Next to me I heard a shout of pain, and Felix dropped to the ground with a spear in the thigh.

But I had not trained for thousands of watches to die at the hands of Goths. I rolled as I hit the ground and came half erect into a crouch, assessing the situation.

The mule was still next to me and I grabbed my newly looted bow and two quivers. From the corner of my eye I saw two Goths with spears bearing down on me. I dropped the quivers, drew my gladius with my left hand and did what comes naturally. When they lay at my feet, bleeding away their life blood onto the frozen soil, I strung the bow, grabbed five arrows from the quiver with my draw hand, and released my first arrow in the same motion. The Goth crumpled at my feet, falling next to the injured Felix.

I regained my composure and as I looked up, I saw Hostilius going down onto one knee, losing the fight against three huge Goths. They died nearly instantaneously. My looted bow was a masterpiece. Not a Hunnic bow, but still incredibly powerful. I was shooting at extreme close range - twenty paces, maybe thirty. An arrow shot from a composite bow at twenty paces hits with the force equivalent to that of a war hammer. I had to use the broad-headed hunting arrows as I had no time to modify them.

The first arrow split the skull of the closest Goth, the second penetrated the rib cage of another attacker. The third arrow passed right through the neck of Hostilius's only remaining adversary, almost decapitating him.

All around me Goths attacked the century with devastating effect, but I was only warming up. My eyes found two Goths running at Ursa with their spears held horizontally. They died.

I turned to my left and one by one released sixty arrows in double the number of heartbeats. My last arrow was still airborne when I dropped the bow and drew my gladius. I lost count of the bodies. I was in no mood for mercy after what happened to Bellus and Felix.

When the Goths withdrew into the undergrowth, forty-three of them lay dead or dying, arrows protruding from heads, necks and torsos.

An eerie silence descended and was broken by Ursa banging his sword on his shield, chanting rhythmically. "Umbra! Umbra! Umbra!"

Within seconds the whole century followed suit, I even noticed Hostilius joining in. He was shaking his head, eyeballing the three dead Goths surrounding him.

The Goths were gone. They executed a surprise attack, killed legionaries and set free many of the prisoners, as well as horses. It was never meant to be a pitched battle. Every century lost men. The two legions lost nearly five hundred soldiers in the attack. Another eighty were seriously wounded.

Once the attack had ended, we immediately turned our attention to the wounded, each contubernium taking care of their own. The Gothic spear had passed through Felix's thigh without severing a major artery or hitting bone. I returned to the pack mule and retrieved my small medical kit that my friend Cai had assembled for me. I told Ursa to hold Felix down and showed Silentus where to grip the spear. With a powerful blow I severed the spear shaft at the entry point. Felix's body shuddered in pain. Even the giant Ursa struggled to hold him down.

They braced again and I extracted the shaft from the wound, which started to bleed freely. I cleaned the wound with vinegar and applied honey and a herb paste in the way that Cai had taught me. I cut a piece of clean cloth from my spare tunic and bound the wound expertly.

Pumilio stared at me wide-eyed. "I suppose that if you mete out wounds that regularly, it's good to know how to fix 'em", he said.

Felix was placed on a wagon and Hostilius accompanied him to ensure that he would receive the best treatment.

Incidentally, I later heard that the ambush and the losses were never communicated to the senate in Rome. The only official record of the campaign was a crushing defeat inflicted on the Scythians by the soldier emperor. Maximinus Thrax may have been a barbarian by birth, but he was learning the ways of Rome.

We crossed the Danube late that afternoon and arrived back at the temporary camp garrisoned by the Legio II Adiutrix.

Our overwhelming victory against the Yazyges were clouded by the heavy losses we sustained during the ambush. There was a sombre atmosphere in the camp.

Since we were on Roman soil and the hostilities had ceased, each contubernium was allowed to deal with its own deceased comrades.

We found a quiet spot close to the river and built a funeral pyre for Bellus.

We laid him on his shield and watched as the flames consumed his body.

Silentus collected his ashes in a clay vase to deliver back to his family in Rome.

Bellus's shade was journeying Elysium because he had received a proper burial, but for him to live forever we had to honour his memory.

We went back to camp and lit a fire. We still had raw meat left from the previous evening and soon it was sizzling over the coals. Each of us told stories of the deeds of Bellus to ensure his arrival in Elysium.

Hostilius joined us later in the evening. He carried an amphora of wine instead of his vine cane. That night he was one of us, and he joined in to celebrate the memories of a fallen comrade.

In the absence of Felix, I read Bellus's will.

His coin and his sword would go to his family who lived on a farm in the Province. Hostilius would arrange it.

His helmet, as his most prized possession, inscribed with his name, would go to Silentus. Although they did not speak much due to Silentus's issues, we learned that they were friends during their youth and joined the legions on the same day.

There were not enough coins in the funeral club to have a proper stone carved in his memory. Hostilius and I both contributed to pay a stonemason for a simple stone.

"Bellus served the Legio IV Italica for twelve years.

He was born on a Monday, joined the army on a Tuesday, and died on a Wednesday.

His first scar was also his last.

His comrades vow to preserve his memory."

The stone is still there, all these years later. I visit it often.

Chapter 12 – Centurion (September 236 AD)

Having achieved victory, we were granted a day of rest.

There was nowhere to go, so we ended up spending the day next to the fire. We repaired our damaged gear, cleaned our armour and whetted our swords.

Around the middle of the afternoon I received a message to report to Hostilius. It was unexpected and I had no idea what it was about. I opened the door and his secretary waved me through to his quarters without saying a word.

Head Tribune Cornelius Carbo was sitting with the centurion, sharing an amphora of wine. I immediately came to attention and saluted.

Hostilius gestured to the remaining chair. "Remember it is your day off, legionary, come share some wine with us."

He drank deeply from his cup, looked at Carbo and continued. "I submitted my report to the tribune this morning. The emperor was curious why it is that so many Goths met their demise at the hands of the first century of the third cohort. We killed more of the bastards than the rest of the legion put together. The emperor is no patrician. He rewards service rather than birth."

"Congratulations Domitius, you have been promoted to centurion by direct order of the emperor", Hostilius concluded.

I was stunned into silence, and did not know what to say. Hostilius smiled a rare smile, rose from his chair, and clasped my forearm in the way of the soldier. "And don't expect me to thank you every time you save my arse. This time I will, and by the way, both Carbo and I seconded your appointment."

"It is unheard of that a recruit is promoted to centurion so soon", Carbo added. "The veterans will be inclined to reject your authority."

I nodded, understanding the dilemma.

"But after your performance yesterday, every decanus of the contubernia in my century came to me to request that you be rewarded with a promotion. They would follow you anywhere after saving their lives yesterday, Centurion", Hostilius stated.

"I am honoured", I replied, and inclined my head to Carbo and Hostilius in turn.

"You will be centurion of the fifth century of the first cohort", Carbo said.

He had me confused and I said: "Please explain, Tribune."

Allow me to digress. The first cohort is the senior cohort of a legion. Normally, only the veteran centurions would command the double strength centuries of the first cohort.

"You are not the only one who has been promoted, Domitius", Carbo replied. "Centurion Hostilius Proculus is now the head centurion of the first century of the first cohort. His predecessor was killed by a Gothic spear during the attack."

"I insisted that you oversee the weapons training of the first cohort", Hostilius commanded. "Carbo saw the corpses of the Goths surrounding our century and he was initially reluctant to believe that one man could have killed so many."

Hostilius grinned at Carbo and said: "When he saw the truth of it, he was more than adamant that you join the first."

Carbo nodded. "Now that we have defeated the barbarians", he said, "we will be heading back to Sirmium where we will spend the rest of the winter to bring the legion back to full strength. We need to re-organize the legion as a whole to ensure that it remains an effective fighting force."

"As a reward for saving our lives, I will transfer your contubernium to the fifth of the first", Hostilius said.

Carbo nodded in agreement. "Hostilius is now the lead centurion of the legion. It is his decision to make."

I swallowed the last of my wine.

"Domitius, you are dismissed", Hostilius said. "I will make your appointment official on our return to our winter camp in Sirmium. Go tell your contubernium and celebrate."

I saluted them both and left. The feeling was indescribable. I thought that I would spend years as a legionary. Never in my wildest dreams did I think that I would be promoted to centurion within a year.

Hostilius had told my contubernium of my promotion in advance. When I arrived back, they all jumped up, came to attention, and saluted.

I grinned, shook my head and laughed. "You people are insufferable. Why didn't you tell me?"

Ursa had already poured a cup from the large amphora of wine. I identified it as originating from Hostilius's stash, and realised that he had a hand in it.

Pumilio slapped my back. "You deserve this, little brother. If it weren't for you we would all be sitting in Charon's boat, taking a ride across the river Styx."

Silentus nodded in agreement and one after the other they clasped my forearm.

They spent some of the coin they had looted from the multitude of dead Goths to purchase a sheep. We feasted late into the night on spitted mutton and red wine.

In some respects I was also sad, deep inside, knowing that I was now moving on. I would never again be able to feast with them as comrades, equals. I was to be their centurion and I would be responsible for their lives.

We arrived back at Sirmium three weeks later. The temporary camp was intact as we had left it.

Felix had recovered enough during the journey to be released from the care of the medici.

He was walking with the aid of a crutch and I had my doubts whether he would heal well enough to continue serving.

A couple of days later Hostilius summoned me to his quarters. I had been given prior warning to appear in my full military garb.

Hostilius was waiting for me, and as I arrived he said: "Walk with me."

We walked in the direction of the Praetorium. Head Tribune Carbo had called a meeting which the officers of the legion were required to attend.

When all were present he said: "At ease".

Carbo was a hard man, but he was fair and had earned the respect of his men. There was no need to ask for silence. His face said 'shut up'.

As silence descended, he said: "You are here to be told who I have decided to promote. The die is cast. Should you be discontent, you better keep it to yourself."

He announced the appointment of Hostilius, and as the first spear walked forward, the officers cheered loudly. Hostilius Proculus was well respected.

Hostilius announced the rest of the reshuffling of officers, as well as new appointments, which was generally well received. The announcement of my appointment was met with a few murmurs, which ended abruptly when Hostilius mentioned that it was requested by the emperor for bravery.

It is one thing to complain about the actions of a tribune, however, criticising the emperor is treason, carrying with it a reward of immediate execution.

With the announcements finalised, we were dismissed. I turned around to go back to my unit when I felt a hand on my shoulder. It was Hostilius.

"The job of every centurion is to communicate the changes to his century. Once this is done, the changes takes place. I will give the order first thing tomorrow morning", Hostilius said.

He paused for a moment. "Centurion Domitius, there is however one responsibility that I want you to take care of. Felix is no longer fit for duty. He has served for nearly thirty years and is eligible for an honorary discharge. He will receive the full pension that he is due. Go talk to him and tell him that his time in the legions has come to an end."

I would have preferred that he asked me to bring him the scalps of ten Goths before the start of the third watch. Felix's whole life was the legion. He had nowhere to go and no family to return to.

Some say that the gods are cruel, but I have never experienced life that way. I believe that he gods work with us like a master ironsmith works with a sword. He starts with an iron ingot. He does not stroke and caress it into the shape of a sword. He heats the iron and then pounds it over and over until all the impurities have gone. The process is violent and dirty, but the sword that eventually emerges is a masterpiece.

When I walked back to my quarters, I had to focus on calming myself by breathing deeply, not unlike preparing for a battle. Then the gods gave me direction. An idea was planted in my mind and I felt at peace.

Felix was putting a shine on his well-used lorica segmentata. Due to his immobility he was the only one of the contubernium who remained in the camp. We were given the afternoon off from duty and the rest of the men had gone into town. No doubt that they were already deep into their cups.

I sat down opposite Felix once I had retrieved a small amphora of red wine that I had recently procured in Sirmium. Did I mention that good red wine was one of the things I spent my coin on? That, and anything related to weapons and war. In any event, I opened the wine and poured two cups.

He swallowed deeply and smacked his lips. "Did Hostilius send you?" he asked.

Felix had been in the army long enough, and he was no fool.

"Yes", I replied.

He nodded. "I know that it is not your decision, you are only the messenger", he said.

He drained the rest of his cup and I followed suit.

I filled the cups again. "Felix, may I ask how you came to serve in the legions?" I asked.

"I have never told the boys how I ended up in the legions, but I might as well tell you. You saved my life twice over. First you killed those Goths and then you took care of my wound. By the gods, all of us owe you our lives", Felix said.

It was late afternoon and darkness was descending over the camp. Felix turned his cup in his calloused hands as if trying to find the words in the wine.

"My father owned a farm close to Rome", he sighed. "I was raised on that farm. We worked hard and we did well, or rather, I thought we did well. My parents could even afford a tutor to teach us our letters and numbers, although the old Greek was half drunk most of the time and probably came cheap. My father and mother were good people, but somehow they borrowed coin from the wrong man."

"The man they had borrowed from coveted our farm. Rich, powerful and influential men get what they want, eh?"

He took a deep swallow from his cup and continued, a deep frown on his weathered face.

He stared into the distance. "I can remember it as if it happened yesterday. I was in the kitchen lighting a fire for my mother when they arrived. We knew nothing of it. Apparently the farm was taken as payment for settlement of the debt, and the men had come to evict us. A fat official and two ruffians from the city."

"My mother told them to leave the house, and the official struck her."

He looked me in the eye. "My grandfather was in the legions, and he had taught me how to work a blade before the coughing sickness took him. I was not close to as good as you are, but who is, eh?"

"They struck my mother and they died. All three of them. What can I say, I was young."

"That's how my father found us heartbeats later. I left the farm that same afternoon. Never been back."

"The great Septimius Severus was recruiting for his campaign in Britannia and two months later we were camped next to the fortified wall built by Emperor Hadrianus. I later heard that my father was executed and my mother sold into slavery in some obscure part of the Empire. I thought about deserting to try and find her."

He stared down at his feet and said: "But I was too afraid of execution if I did, so I did nothing, nothing. And now it's too late."

"I got no family, no skills, nowhere to go." He smiled weakly and added: "I guess that's the fate of most of us old timers, so I shouldn't really feel special."

I rolled the dice. "What did your father farm with?" I asked.

"Horses", he replied.

I smiled then, which I could see confused him.

"I have a proposal for you, Felix", I said as I refilled our cups for the third time.

Chapter 13 – Optio

As I had mentioned earlier, if you follow the path laid out by the gods, things fall into place.

Early the next morning the whole contubernium packed their belongings in order to relocate. The same thing was happening all over the camp as the legion restructured.

For the first time I dressed in the garb of a centurion which was issued to me the previous day. I donned my transverse horsehair crest and brand new metal greaves. My friends had helped me polish my chain mail to a brilliant shine, and I certainly looked the part. And I carried a vine cane, of course.

Hostilius came to fetch the group that were to join the first century. We took our neatly packed belongings and followed him. The items we could not carry were stacked on the pack mule.

He had allowed Felix to join us, as he still had a few weeks left before his official discharge. He was on light duty, though, which meant that he mostly stayed in the vicinity of our accommodations, and kept the fire going.

The Primus Pilus escorted me to my new quarters. Centurions did not share accommodations, I had my own room. I was also allowed to employ a slave or a servant if I wished to.

Once I had placed my belongings in my quarters, I was taken to my new century, the fifth of the first.

Unlike the previous day, with Felix, I was not nervous at all. In my past life, east of the Danube, I had regularly commanded a thousand Huns and had even killed a rebellious subordinate in a duel.

Roman legionaries are trained to do many things, but above all, the legions were designed around a system which enforced strict discipline. It was the most important differentiation between the legions and its barbarian counterparts. Discipline.

The benefit of this culture for a centurion, or any other officer, is that you are obeyed. It does not matter whether one is a good or bad officer. The punishment for not obeying a command from your senior is severe.

In any event, Hostilius called an assembly of the fifth century of the first cohort. He introduced me as the new centurion while the men were standing at attention – a double strength century of one hundred and sixty battle-hardened veterans, eyeing me with suspicion.

Amongst the hostile faces I spied Felix, Pumilio, Ursa and Silentus. It made me feel at ease.

I was never one for speeches and I said: "You are now my century and I am responsible for your actions, by command of the emperor. We are all here to do our duty to Rome. Dismissed."

Hostilius nodded in agreement and left to attend to his duties.

Many young men dream of one day becoming a centurion in the legions. They imagine the life of a warrior, slaying the enemies of Rome and eventually retiring a hero.

That is far from the truth. I soon realised that the bulk of the work is administration - setting up duty rosters, arranging the watch list and writing daily reports to Hostilius.

Administration and keeping the peace. One hundred tough, mostly uneducated men crammed into a confined space is a recipe for conflict. Add another fifty-eight centuries, slaves, auxiliaries and camp followers, and you have trouble aplenty.

There is one remedy that I discovered rather quickly. Men, even the rough men of the legions, are less prone to cause mischief when they are exhausted.

I had personal experience of this, inflicted upon me by my barbarian tutor, Bradakos.

I made them run and do weapons training in full armour.

Our stints were longer and more intensive than that of any other century, the only difference being that I participated in every activity rather than just meting out punishment.

Very soon my nickname changed to Belua, which means "monster". I cared little.

Every centurion has a second in charge. The position is referred to as the "chosen man", or optio. This position is normally a stepping stone to the rank of centurion and comes with various responsibilities as well as double pay. My predecessor was killed and his optio had to retire due to the loss of three fingers on his sword hand.

I had the consent of Hostilius to first evaluate the men before proposing a candidate.

At first I was tempted to choose one of the men from my previous contubernium, but that would be seen as favouritism and only cause more problems than it solved.

Didius Castus caught my attention from the outset. Physically he was intimidating, yet spoke little. He excelled at weapons training and was an excellent swordsman. I often used him to demonstrate a technique to the century. He was slow to anger, yet respected as he had put more than one of his comrades on the injury list when harassed. He was literate, albeit not to a very high level, but more than sufficient to read and write reports and do basic numbers work.

He had always been overlooked for promotion due to his one major drawback. He possessed a terrible stutter, which was not always present, but reared its head from time to time.

I must say, it took more than a little effort to convince Hostilius to sanction his appointment, but in the end he agreed, although reluctantly.

Once I possessed the mandate, I called Didius to my office. He walked up to my desk, saluted smartly and came to attention, focusing his gaze on some imaginary spot above my right shoulder. His armour was meticulously maintained.

"Hand me your gladius, legionary", I said.

I could clearly see on his face that I had confused him with the request, but he nonetheless complied immediately by drawing his shortsword and offering it to me, hilt first.

I studied the blade intently. It was extremely well taken care of. The edge was perfect and I tested it for sharpness by shaving the hairs on my forearm.

I handed the blade back to him and he sheathed it immediately, coming to attention as I said: "Congratulation Didius, you are now the optio of the fifth of the first. At ease."

He was speechless. In the back of my mind I hoped that it was not due to the inability to form the words, but rather due to the surprise that I had sprung.

He regained his composure and replied: "I am honoured, sir."

"When in private, call me Umbra or Lucius," I said, and smiled. "I prefer that to Belua."

His face turned light red and he said: "I understand sir…sorry, Umbra."

I spent some time with him, setting out my expectations.

Later the same day I called my century to assemble, and true to my commitment to short speeches, said: "I have appointed Didius Castus as my optio."

As arranged with Didius, he came forward and accepted the hastile, a five feet staff, from me as a sign of his authority.

I left the parade ground and thereby passed the control of the century to Didius. He gave the order for the men to fall out and I could hear the congratulations being offered to the new optio by his former comrades. I felt good about my decision.

The feeling didn't last long.

Early the following morning we assembled outside the fort for additional weapons training. I was not at all content with the way that the century cast their iron-tipped spears.

The idea is for the spears to impact more or less at the same spot along the line. Putting it differently, the stronger throwers needed to tone it down slightly and the weaker ones needed to improve.

We had been working on this for nearly a watch in separate groups when we re-assembled as a unit. I decided to get

Didius to command the century to allow me to see where the mistakes were made.

The century stood in line, three men deep and fifty men wide.

Didius looked decidedly uncomfortable, which I attributed to the fact that he was new to the position.

He voice was impressively loud as he shouted: "Century, release p… p… p…"

He started again: "Century, release p…"

I intervened. "Century release pila", I boomed.

Predictably, what followed was a disaster, but nonetheless some of the rankers had grins on their faces.

I am ashamed to say that what followed was one of the few moments during my time as a centurion that I laid into the men with my vine cane. Although they bore the brunt of my anger, I was irritated with myself for appointing Didius.

Didius just stood there, forlornly, not really knowing how to react.

Fortunately I regained my composure within a reasonably short time and we spent the rest of the day on the training ground perfecting the manoeuvre. Needless to say, I relieved Didius from giving the verbal command.

We marched back to the camp at dusk and I asked Didius to join me at my quarters to share the evening meal.

I poured two generous cups of neat red wine and I emptied mine in one long satisfying gulp. Didius followed suit.

Once the wine had taken the edge off the day's proceedings, I sat down behind my desk and motioned to Didius to take a chair.

One of the options foremost in my mind was to accept that I had made a mistake with Didius and to appoint a more suitable candidate.

Didius sat down, but before I could speak, he said: "I am sorry Centurion. I will understand if you wish to replace me as your chosen man."

I hesitated for a moment, which probably gave away my original thoughts.

"It only h… h… happens when I get nervous", he stuttered.

But I had made up my mind with Didius's original statement. "Don't be concerned Didius. Starting today, I will teach you to breathe", I replied.

He stared at me as if I had lost my mind and made the revelation. "But I already know how to breathe?"

Chapter 14 – Visit

It took two months to get the stutter under control, but it felt like a year.

Finally my century was functioning normally. Their skills at the stakes had also increased markedly. I trained daily with Didius and he was becoming one of the best swordsmen in the cohort.

Felix's discharge was imminent. All the necessary documents had been signed and approved, so I went to speak with Hostilius to explain my plan regarding Felix.

He approved and agreed to attend Felix's send-off. I had booked an exclusive evening at Felix's favourite establishment in Sirmium, not exactly a drinking hole, but only slightly more upmarket. It was called the Thirsty Mule.

I remember the evening well. How I managed it, I would never know, but I drank sparingly. I guess the quality of the wine was a major contributor.

During the first half of the evening I spent my time with Ursa, Pumilio and Silentus, listening to their recollections of Felix's endeavours. When they were too deep into their cups to speak coherently, I rather talked with Felix and Hostilius, who were holding out surprisingly well.

Hostilius had served with Felix for many years, and he approved three days of leave to enable me to execute my plan.

I was up before first light. I expected that I would struggle to rouse Felix, but to my surprise he was waiting for me outside my room, with his few possessions neatly packed. As I had little baggage, I picked up half and we started off without saying a word. Felix had said his last goodbyes the evening before and I think that he was not keen to say goodbye a second time, especially while being sober.

We presented our official passes at the gate and left for Sirmium, which was less than half a mile distant.

The gates of the town were open already. I was in full uniform, so we had no trouble gaining entry, and the watch officer even saluted as we walked through.

I headed directly for the area dedicated to the horse traders. A fair number of the horses that we had taken from the Yazyges as the spoils of war ended up with traders in Sirmium.

As a result we were spoilt for choice. I insisted that Felix select his own horse, provided it was a mare. While he was inspecting the available horses, I went to the shops of the saddlers, which were close to the stables.

I had mentioned before that I am not a man who spends his coin on trinkets or clothes, but when it comes to items of war or horses, I am not shy to part with gold.

Felix was the man who had welcomed me into the legion and showed me many of the little proverbial tricks of the trade.

I felt indebted to him, and therefore I purchased the best saddle I could find. There were many ornate examples, but I ended up purchasing a beautiful one, my decision based on quality and craftsmanship.

While the excited saddler made a few adjustments to the item, I went to see what Felix was up to.

I found him making friends with a magnificent specimen. The mare was clearly a horse bred by the Roxolani. Blonde in colour with a dark brown mane and tail. Based on his selection, it was clear that Felix knew horses, and my mind was set at ease regarding my decision.

I left Felix to cement the friendship while I went to negotiate the purchase. The horse did obviously not come cheap, but as part of the deal I had convinced the trader to loan me a horse for our trip home.

We collected the saddle and similarly I received an old worn saddle on loan for a day or two.

As we rode out the gates of Sirmium, I said to Felix: "The horse and the saddle is a gift, although, should we breed with her, the offspring is mine."

Felix suddenly spurred his new horse and galloped down the road. I was not surprised - he did not wish for me to see the tears in his eyes.

I eventually caught up with a smiling Felix. "Umbra, I feel like you have given me back a part of my youth, thank you."

I nodded. "You extended the hand of friendship to me, Felix. That is worth even more."

We ended up discussing the farm and what I wanted to achieve. I explained to him that I aimed to breed a horse that was softer on the eye than the Hun horses, and larger, but still retaining some of the traits that make the Hun horses ideal for a military application.

Less that a watch later, we approached the farm, which I had not seen for close on nine moons.

As we were either on campaign or training, I did not write, nor did I receive letters. Maybe it is just an excuse, but I have never been fond of writing or reading letters, which Nik and Cai were aware of.

Felix was excited to see the outlandish Hunnic horses for the first time, while I was anxious about the wellbeing of my family, especially my father.

We were less than a mile away from the farm when I saw four of the Roxolani guards galloping towards us at an angle. They obviously wanted to intercept us before we reached the villa. I was wearing my legionary garb, with my helmet hanging from my saddle. I noticed that the warriors had arrows nocked and were steering the horses with their legs. Next to me I could see the confusion and concern on Felix's face.

"Rein in, Felix. Leave this to me. And don't touch your sword", I said.

Felix and I came to a complete stop, with the barbarians thundering towards us. When they were fifty yards away, they suddenly reined in and stored their bows.

They trotted up to us and all four of them dismounted. The leader grinned broadly as he walked up to me and said in passable Latin: "Welcome home, lord."

"It is good to see you too, Karsas", I said.

His eyes drifted to Felix and I said in Scythian: "This is a friend of mine."

Karsas smiled and again replied in Latin: "A friend of Prince Eochar is friend of Roxolani."

The warriors mounted again and galloped towards the gate.

Felix looked at me sideways. "What's with this 'lord' and 'prince' when they speak to you?"

"They are still learning Latin, Felix. They mean to say 'sir'", I explained.

With that I spurred my borrowed horse and galloped towards the gates of the villa.

My father and Cai were waiting for us when we walked our horses through the gate.

Felix and I dismounted, and I handed the reins of my horse to a Roxolani. He looked at my horse in a critical, confused way, until I cleared it up by saying in Scythian: "It's a loan horse." He nodded, smiled in understanding, and led the animal away.

I introduced Felix to Nik and Cai.

My father placed his hand on my shoulder. "I have instructed the servants to prepare hot water for you and your friend", he said. "When you are refreshed we will get together to celebrate, Centurion." I smiled, because my father's mind was still as sharp as ever - he immediately deduced my rank from my military dress.

We both enjoyed a relaxing hot bath and dressed in clean tunics and cloaks.

I went to my own room, which had been cleaned by servants during my bath. My bows, sword and armour were prominently displayed just as I had left them. I drew the jian blade from its scabbard and noticed that it had been expertly polished and maintained.

Similarly, my bows and armour had been meticulously oiled. Cai had been busy.

I lay down on the bed and savoured the privacy and comfort of my own home, which I had voluntarily abandoned for a life in the legions. Had I made a foolish decision out of boredom?

Before my thoughts progressed too far down that avenue, there was a knock on the door and Nik peeked in. I motioned for him to sit down on the bed.

He sat down slowly, as the bed was lower than a chair, and sighed: "I guess my age is finally catching up to me."

"Nik, don't be ridiculous, you will never be old", I said and it made him smile.

"I did not expect you to write", he said. "Life in the legions is busy and filled with intrigue."

He placed his arm on my shoulder and suddenly I felt like a boy again, waiting to hear a bedtime story. I guess Nik shared that thought with me and he said: "The difference is, Lucius, this time you do the talking and I listen." Then he added: "Cai and the warriors are showing your friend around the farm, we will feast later."

I told him about the happenings during the months I had been away. He listened intently, interrupting me many times to extract a more detailed account. I marvelled at the comments of my father, showing his deep insight into the thoughts of men. I had to remind myself that this old man once called a Roman Emperor his friend and mingled with barbarian kings.

In any event, I could see that he was immensely proud of my achievements.

"Lucius, I am content on the farm. I enjoy working with the horses. I know you will never return permanently and Cai is travelling another path. I have been trying to find a reliable man to assist me, but I have not been able to find one."

I couldn't help smiling, which made my father frown. I explained my plan regarding Felix and soon we were having a chuckle.

"Lucius, the older one gets, the more one sees the hands of the gods in our lives, but surely even you can see it today."

The patricians in Rome would never degrade themselves by preparing their own food. To even be in the vicinity when food is prepared is not ideal, as the smell of the food permeates clothing.

Unlike the city folk, my father loved nothing more than to sit out in the open next to a fire.

Our barbarian guards spitted a wild boar and a sheep over a purpose-built stone pit. I sat close by with Nik, Cai and Felix, sipping on the best wine I have had in years.

"Nik, where do you get this?" I said.

"Son, I still know people in Rome with farms in Gaul. These wealthy senators meticulously prepare wine for their own consumption using only the best grapes. This particular red has been aged for seventeen years. You know, I had to resort to blackmail to be able to lay my hands on this."

Felix thought it a jest and we all laughed heartily. Knowing my father, I was not so sure and I saw the glint in Nik's eye.

I explained to them that Felix knew of horses, and that he would manage the farm in exchange for one fifth of the profits from the farming operation. He would also stay in the main house and dine for free. This I had agreed with Felix beforehand so letting Nik and Cai know was a mere formality.

Felix was impressed with what he had seen during the tour of the farm. He marvelled at the Hunnic horses and was amazed at their hardiness and abilities.

"I can't wait to start working with the horses. Although I have not done it for years, it is still in my blood. Thank you again."

The following day I spent mostly in the company of my father. We went hunting with bow and arrow, but it was just a pretence for enjoying one another's company. I did manage to kill a couple of wild fowl, though.

That evening I dined with my friends again. We enjoyed the fowl with cheese and olives, obviously accompanied by my father's best vintage.

I knew I would be leaving the next morning early and I tried to make the most of it. I still remember it fondly as one of the best evenings of my life.

Chapter 15 – Servant

I rose early with a heavy heart.

Life on the farm was not for me, that I knew, but leaving my friends and my father behind was difficult.

Sirmium was not far away, but I still wanted to leave early, just in case I ran into some kind of difficulty.

In any event, I shared some bread, cheese and olives with Nik, and walked to the stables to ready my horse for the trip.

I was surprised to find Cai waiting for me in the courtyard. He was seemingly also ready to leave.

I turned to Nik, trying to gauge what was happening, but his face was an emotionless mask.

"Don't look at me, Lucius, ask him yourself", my father said.

I sighed asking the question, already knowing the answer. "Where are you going, Cai?"

"I was told to go with you. I your new servant and clerk", he said.

I turned around to Nik with a questioning look.

His face still wore a blank expression and he said: "I told you. I have nothing to do with it."

Cai now had a scowl on his face. "Let's go, you wasting time", he said.

Nik said: "Cai told me a few days ago you would come home and that he would go with you. Don't worry about us. Felix and I have a lot of gossip to catch up on."

I noticed that Cai had my bows and the jian sword strapped to the back of his packhorse. I didn't even try to argue with the little monk. I knew that I could never win.

"Good. Acceptance of one's fate is first step towards enlightenment", he said and winked.

I scowled. "Cai, I am sure you make these things up as you go along", I replied.

With that I embraced my father, clasped arms with Felix, and vaulted onto my borrowed horse.

We were well on our way when I noticed four amphorae of wine strapped to the rear of the packhorse.

Cai noticed my gaze. "Life too short to drink bad wine", he said. "I leave your cloak behind to make space for wine. Wine also help to make warm, so no loss."

We reached Sirmium mid-morning and I returned the loan horse and saddle. I sold the packhorse for some coin. As an officer of the legion, I was allowed to stable a horse at no cost.

The legion was not only brilliant at making war, it was as good at administration. Everything that happened had to be recorded. On our arrival, I was allowed into the camp based on my written leave orders, signed by Hostilius.

I stabled Cai's horse, which I declared as my property, and it was recorded as such. I was handed a written receipt.

Cai and I then went to see Hostilius's clerk to enter Cai's name into the legionary register as a servant and clerk assigned to myself. He received a small metal plaque inscribed with his name and unit, to be worn around his neck at all times.

Once we had taken care of the paperwork, we retired to my quarters to unpack.

Cai told me to boil water so that he could prepare tea. I philosophically pondered who the servant was, and who the master.

While the vile-smelling concoction was brewing, he said: "Nik told me you met emperor."

I nodded and he continued: "Your council of elders, the senate, as you Romans call it, despise him. They fear him. They too afraid to stand up to him."

"Cai, he is a soldier, not a politician. He has already defeated the Marcomanni and the Quadi on the Rhine, and the Carpi and Goths on the Danube. Rome needs a soldier to ensure that the borders of the Empire is safe."

Cai sipped some of the evil herbal brew and passed me a small cup. Again I accepted, resigned to my new fate.

"Lucius of the Da Qin, soldier never survive in politics. The Da Qin need soldier who is also politician."

"Cai, it is a rare commodity", I replied.

He sipped his tea and gave me the 'drink your tea' look.

I drank deeply, not daring to breathe through my nose, avoiding most of the aroma.

"Yet you had many who both", Cai said. "Julius Ceasar, Marcus Aurelius?"

"Yet again you are correct, Cai of the Serica. But the likes of those men do not come around that often."

I remember Cai just staring at me for a while. Then he said: "I listen to Nik and see that storm is gathering. Just like it happen in land of Serica. Lucius, you must prepare for storm. Be careful not associate too close with emperor."

He took another swallow. "I see enough of Goths to know that across Danube storm clouds gather as well. Do what you need to weather storm."

Cai had a way of speaking in riddles. I knew better than to try to extract more information from him.

"Thank you, Cai. I will heed your warning, although I will pray to the gods to guide me."

The next morning it was back to army life. The only difference being that Cai made me a hearty breakfast of fried smoked pork, hard cheese and freshly baked flatbread. He also forced me to drink some brewed potion, which he conveniently referred to as tea.

I dedicated more time to weapons training than other centurions. It was the second watch of the morning and my century was at the stakes, practising a manoeuvre repeatedly, where a feint thrust is made at head height, followed by an angled upward punch with the scutum, and finished off with a powerful straight thrust to the lower legs of the opponent. I had them repeat it until I was satisfied with the level of intensity and with the timing. Only then did I allow the men to rest.

A legionary summoned me to report to Hostilius immediately. I handed over to Didius, my optio, and marched back to the camp.

Hostilius was seated at his desk. He wore a scowl and his face was red, although it was far from hot outside.

I came to attention and saluted. He began to speak and with the wave of his hand indicated that I could stand at ease.

"I have just received marching orders from Tribune Carbo. The first and second cohorts and half the cavalry are heading out tomorrow morning at first light. We will be escorting Maximinus Thrax. Our destination is Noviodunum ad Istrum, close to where the Danube flows into the Dark Sea."

Hostilius sighed. "The reason why I am telling you first is that you will be delivering a message to the king of the Goths on behalf of the emperor. Pack what you need."

He dismissed me, and I heard him arrange a meeting with the other centurions of the first and second cohorts.

As a centurion, I was allocated my own mule and a small cart. I could take all my weapons and armour. We even had space for some of the wine that Nik had given us.

I spent the evening walking from tent to tent conversing with the men. I felt that their attitude in general had improved.

I took some of Nik's wine to share with my old contubernium.

The wine loosened their tongues. "The boys heard what you did for Felix", Ursa said. "You are feared throughout the legion, Umbra - they all know what happened when the Goths attacked us. But now they respect you 'cause you look after oldsters like Felix."

"What have you heard about where we are going?" I asked.

Pumilio scowled and whispered: "A little bird told me the emperor wants to use gold to pay off the Goths. Things like this make the men unhappy. We would rather go kill the Goths and the emperor can give us the gold. We thought the Thracian was a soldier, but now we don't know anymore."

Ursa looked around to make sure no one was listening. "He got to be careful. When Emperor Alexander and his mother paid off the Germani, the men got angry and it ended badly."

I could see that the discussion was not going well and I said: "The walls have ears, watch what you say."

Ironically, Silentus nodded in agreement.

Chapter 16 – The road east (February 237 AD)

Two cohorts left camp at first light.

The emperor and his bodyguards formed the vanguard, followed by the cavalry. I noticed that my friend Marcus was amongst the riders.

I heard that we would travel east on the Via Militaris for six hundred miles, and that the journey would take slightly longer than a moon.

I was walking with my century when Hostilius slowed down to speak with me.

"Domitius, have you ever been as far east as the shores of the Dark Sea?" he asked.

"Yes Primus Pilus, I have", I replied.

"How far east have you been?"

"I would think, as the crow flies, about three thousand miles east and north of where we are now."

Hostilius did not reply for a while, but kept on marching. "Is that where your servant comes from? I have heard that he is from the land of Serica."

"No sir, to reach the land of Serica you still need to travel three thousand miles farther east. It is not only the distance that is an obstacle. Between Scythia and the land of Serica live the most fearsome of barbarians."

I thought for a moment and added: "Some of them even eat their vanquished enemies."

Hostilius looked at me suspiciously. Yet from experience, he knew I spoke plainly.

"Domitius, suddenly I feel better about meeting the Goths. At least I won't be on the menu."

I motioned to him and we walked out of hearing distance of the men. "Primus Pilus, there is a rumour among the ranks that the emperor is travelling to the Goths to pay them a bribe to leave us alone. It does not sit well with the men, and neither with me."

"The emperor is despised by the senate", Hostilius replied. "He has the blood of barbarians flowing through his veins. The senate wishes one of their own to be emperor. A Roman noble. They are planting the seeds of revolt amongst the legions. Only the emperor can root it out, but not while he is fighting a war against the Goths. I do not agree with paying them off, but I understand why he is doing it."

I replied, maybe too hastily, but I had come to trust and respect Hostilius. "We should cross the Danube and crush the Goths. We will find many allies among the Scythian tribes who despise the Goths and would be willing to fight at our side. The Goths cannot be trusted."

"My mother's people, the Roxolani, had made peace with the Goths, but they broke the blood oath which is sacred to the people of the Sea of Grass. They will take the gold of the emperor and use it to buy more warriors to kill Romans."

"I agree with you, Domitius, but it is not our decision", Hostilius answered. "We are here to follow orders."

I think he was testing me to see whether I possessed a mutinous streak, but I nonetheless told him what was in my heart.

"Primus Pilus, the strength of the legions is its discipline. Although I do not agree with the emperor, I will do as I am commanded. We cannot all be emperors."

Hostilius slapped me on the back and quickened his pace to catch up with his century.

Fortunately we marched along the Via Militaris and most evenings we camped outside the gates of some or other friendly town or military fort. We never had to construct a marching camp, which allowed me to perform weapons training drills with my century nearly every afternoon. When time allowed it, I trained with Cai in the early evening, obviously away from prying eyes.

We eventually arrived in Noviodunum ad Istrum during the last watch of the thirty-fourth day on the road.

Noviodunum was a large fort and was not only the base for the Legio I Italica, but also the headquarters of the Roman fleet operating on the lower Danube.

Thankfully the emperor had arranged lodgings for our two cohorts inside the fort, and we were all settled in before the sun had set.

Not long after, a messenger summoned me to attend to Primus Pilus Hostilius. I left Cai behind to unpack, and followed the messenger.

Hostilius did not mince his words. "Domitius, the emperor wants you to leave first thing in the morning. Your mission is to take a message to the ruler of the Goths and arrange a meeting on the nearby island in the Danube. Unfortunately your rank is not sufficient for such a mission, therefore Tribune Marcus from the cavalry will have to accompany you."

"I would like to take my servant as well", I replied.

Hostilius shrugged. "As you wish, yet it does surprise me that you would need a clerk on such a mission."

"Cai has certain other skills, sir", I replied.

"I see", was all he said in reply.

"You and the tribune will report to me first thing in the morning. I will provide you with the written letter to the Goths, as well as your final orders. Dismissed."

I saluted and departed to find my friend, Tribune Marcus Aurelius Valerius.

He was not present in the officer's quarters and I eventually found him in the stables. We were alone so I addressed him in an informal manner.

"Well met, Marcus", I said after I had sneaked up on him.

He spun around with an annoyed expression, but when he saw me, he embraced me like a brother.

"No doubt you have received your orders", he said. "I have taken the liberty to find you the same horse that you used when we scouted together."

"Thank you, Marcus", I replied. "Could you arrange a horse for Cai as well?"

"Your healer?" Marcus asked. "How come he is in camp?"

"Cai, my friend from the land of Serica, volunteered to be my clerk and servant", I explained.

Marcus just shook his head. "The best healer that I have ever heard of is your servant? I should have expected nothing less."

"Marcus, this mission is extremely dangerous. We will have to reveal ourselves to the Goths and there is no guarantee that they will let us leave. We might end up dead - or even worse, in chains."

Resigned to my fate, I went back to my quarters and informed Cai of our mission. I did not tell him that he was allowed to join me, but he was insistent, to say the least.

I allowed him to suffer for a while, and then told him that I had arranged for him to travel with us.

Cai had prepared a delicious meat stew, and we shared some of Nik's excellent wine.

"Lucius, I see your destiny intertwined with Goths. It may not please you, but sooner you make peace with it, the better."

"Cai, I fear that you are right. In my heart I feel that Arash has tasked me to be the bane of the Goths. I think I can find peace in war."

Cai thought deeply and sipped on his wine. "Wise master from days long ago said it better to be warrior in garden than gardener in war."

"I will think on this, but I have no idea what you are saying", I replied.

Cai smiled slyly and replied: "Lucius of the Da Qin, remember words. Soon you might understand."

Chapter 17 – Old friends

A third of a watch before sunrise Marcus and I met in Hostilius's office, while Cai patiently waited outside with the horses.

Tribune Carbo was present, and he handed Marcus a wooden tube covered with leather. The open end of the tube was secured with the intricate seal of the emperor.

"Tribune and Centurion, you are to deliver this to the ruler of the Goths. You are not to open this or read it. Should the Goths request you to read it, only the tribune is allowed to assist them. The content must not be shared", Carbo commanded.

Cornelius Carbo looked at Marcus, who nodded and confirmed: "I understand and I will obey."

"I understand, Tribune, and I will obey", I said.

Carbo nodded.

"The emperor appreciates the complexity of the mission", he said. "You will travel vast distances through barbarian lands. Remember, the emperor rewards success. Dismissed."

We saluted smartly and departed. Hostilius saluted and then clasped our forearms in the military way.

"May the gods watch over you", he said.

We were allocated two horses each. A Roman military barge was waiting for us at the quayside and discreetly dropped us off on the barbarian side of the river.

We were on a diplomatic mission and therefore we wore our official military dress. In my case I had exchanged my centurion's helmet for a Roman cavalry helmet.

The emperor wished to purchase peace, and he knew that the Goths held the power. Apart from that, the information was sketchy at best.

We watched the barge slowly return to the civilized side of the Danube.

Marcus sighed and said: "Lucius, any suggestions on where we go from here?"

I grinned, as I knew exactly what I wanted to do.

"Marcus, now I go home", I said as I whipped my horse's head around and headed away from the river at a canter.

A confused Marcus caught up with me after a while and fell in beside me.

"Marcus, the Goths, unlike the Scythians, came not from the east but from the Ice Islands across the Sea of the North. Many generations ago they split into two groups. The

Thervingi, which means 'people of the forest', live west of the Dniester. The Greuthungi, which means 'people of the pebble coast', live east of the Dniester, north of the Dark Sea."

"The Thervingi and the Greuthungi speak the same language and they intermarry. They assist each other in times of need, but they also fight from time to time. They are not unlike siblings."

"Who are we supposed to deliver the message to? The Thervingi or the Greuthungi?" Marcus asked.

"We will go to the Thervingi", I replied. "The Greuthungi will not invade through the lands of the Thervingi."

"The leader of the Thervingi is called the iudex, it translates to 'law giver'. We will find him and deliver the message. But we have to take a detour. If we travel north, it would take us through the territory of the Bastarnae. They are the lapdogs of the Goths and they will kill us. We are heading to the lands of the Roxolani - they are my people. We will be able to traverse their lands, and they will assist us."

I knew the approximate location of the Roxolani main camp, but due to their nomadic nature, it could never be a certainty. We made our way west for four days, keeping to the ravines and the valleys. We ate dry rations and made our camp within the protection of dense shrubs or rocky outcrops.

The landscape was becoming increasingly flat - we were travelling onto the Sea of Grass.

On the morning of the fifth day I noticed a group of riders galloping towards us. We must have been seen when we had crested a hill, but there was no other way.

We halted. I soon noticed the familiar straw-coloured horses of the Roxolani, and felt at ease.

Then I realised that Marcus and I wore the clothing of Rome. There was a good chance that we would be killed outright, even before they talked to us.

Hospitality between barbarians did not extend to officers of the Roman Empire.

When the warriors were one hundred paces distant, I dismounted and unsheathed my gladius.

Marcus yelled: "There are at least fifty of them Lucius, you cannot win."

Cai wore a bored expression, which gave me hope, as I always suspected that his religion afforded him a glimpse of the future, which he denied, of course.

"Don't worry my friends, just sit tight", I replied, trying to sound convincing.

At fifty paces the Roxolani had formed a line with their heavy spears levelled at us. The riders and horses were armoured with heavy scale and chain. These were the elite heavy cavalry of my people. I felt immensely proud, but I realised that we needed luck to survive.

I removed my helmet, raised my sword in the air, and rammed the blade into the soil in front of me. I went down on one knee and bowed my head, showing my reverence to Arash, the god of war.

I heard the commander shout orders and the Roxolani reined in, coming to a complete halt fifteen paces away.

The leader slowly walked his horse in my direction and when he reined in a few paces away, I rose and made eye contact.

For a while he looked at me, his enormous stallion moving side to side with pent-up energy, his spear still held level.

Suddenly he rammed the spear into the earth, took off his helmet and dismounted.

He kneeled in front of me and said in Scythian: "Forgive me, Lord Eochar, my life is forfeit. I did not know that it was you."

I raised him to his feet and said: "There is nothing to forgive, Elmanos, son of Masas. You fought at my side when we defeated the Goths. I will never forget it."

"You saved us all, lord", he replied.

"Elmanos, I need to see the king. May I ask that you escort us?"

"Lord Eochar, I would be in trouble with the king should I not."

The Roxolani trotted ahead and Marcus fell in beside me. "I wasn't aware of the fact that the Roxolani revered Romans, Lucius", he said.

"There is a lot you don't know about the Roxolani, Marcus", I said, grinned, and galloped away to mingle with the warriors.

I caught up on a lot of happenings chatting with Elmanos. The most important being the passing of the king. Apsikal was my mother's brother and had been king of the Roxolani during my time in Scythia. He was a good man, and I was deeply saddened.

Bradakos, my mentor, had taken over as king.

The distant cousin and champion of the king, Bradakos, had trained me in the use of weapons for years. Our relationship started off as him being my teacher, but we eventually became friends. Closer than friends, it felt like he was the big brother that I never had.

The Goths had nearly defeated the Roxolani when they broke the sacred blood oath. In the aftermath of the treachery my people were faced with a choice. Accept the oppressive Goths as their overlords, or join the Hunnic federation. They decided on the latter and I played my part when, assisted by the Huns, the Roxolani crushed a huge Gothic army.

But there had been a price. I was earmarked to be the king of my people, but my growing reputation did not sit well with Octar, the high king of the Huns. I was forced to leave Scythia and seek refuge in the lands of Rome.

I was at peace with my decision, as I recognized the hands of the gods in the affair. Arash had guided me to leave the People of the Steppes and join the Roman Empire. I did not understand it, but I accepted it.

I had not seen Bradakos for three years. Although I loved him like a brother, I still felt apprehensive when we approached the main camp of the Roxolani.

The tribe had prospered under the protection of the Huns. Many thousands of tents and wagons sprawled along the floor of the wide valley. We rode between the tents while bands of villagers and children parted, staring wide-eyed at the strange warriors adorned in red.

We came to a halt close to the large tent of the king.

At least six bodyguards moved in between us and the king's tent, barring our way.

Two had arrows nocked and the others' hands were resting on the hilts of their swords. I noticed that the bodyguards' armour was practical, rather than ornate. I could see the hand of my minimalist mentor.

In any event, we dismounted and Elmanos approached the guards. The lead guard drew his weapon and Elmanos said: "Inform the king that these emissaries from Rome are here to see him on urgent business. The king would be extremely upset should the news of their arrival be kept from him."

Elmanos did exactly as we had rehearsed.

A guard disappeared into the tent and appeared again a few heartbeats later.

"The king will see you Elmanos. You may bring the foreigners, but their weapons are to remain outside."

The guards took our weapons and searched us thoroughly for any concealed items.

He was standing next to his throne, neatly attired in scale armour made of horse hooves. Bradakos was ever the warrior.

He turned around and in the dim light I saw the scowl that I knew so well.

He looked at us without recognition in his eyes - then I noticed his gaze drift to me and to Cai.

He turned to his guards and said: "You have done well, leave us."

A guard tried to complain, but Bradakos silenced him with a wave of his hand.

He walked towards me and embraced me. When he withdrew, I could see that, like me, he had tears in his eyes.

I went down onto one knee and my companions followed suit.

"It is good to see you Lord Bradakos", I said.

He grabbed my arm and raised me to my feet. "Don't be ridiculous Eochar, you are my brother."

Bradakos turned towards Elmanos and said: "I thank you for bringing Lord Eochar to me immediately. You have done well and will be rewarded."

"Elmanos, arrange the best accommodation for the friends of Lord Eochar", the king commanded.

The Roxolani warrior nodded and led Marcus and Cai from the tent.

Bradakos sighed heavily as soon as we were alone. I could see that the burden of kingship weighed heavily on him.

"Lucius, when I was chosen to be king in your stead, I felt that you had been done a great disservice. Nowadays I think that you were spared much grief."

"Bradakos, I command fewer than two hundred men in the armies of Rome. Even that is a great burden. To command a nation must be difficult. Yet, I see many children and warriors, and the people appear to be in good spirits."

My mentor grinned and replied: "I didn't say that all is not well, just that it is tiring to be king."

"Eochar, tell me about your time across the river", the king said, and poured me a generous helping of red wine into a silver cup, then filled his own to the brim.

I spent nearly a full watch telling him about my time in the legions. I could see that he was truly interested, especially when I relayed the information about the battles. Bradakos was still a warrior at heart.

Once I had told him all he said: "Eochar, I can see that you have been guided onto a path chosen for you, not by you. I will do all in my power to assist you with your mission."

I held out my empty cup and the king refilled it for me. I took a deep swallow and said: "Tell me what happened to my uncle Apsikal."

"Not long after you had to leave, your Hun friend, Gordas, was recalled by his king. The Huns had a problem in the east. They left us with only three hundred men. It was not a problem, as the Goths was not likely to upset the Huns - they know that we are part of the Hunnic alliance."

The king sneered and continued: "But the Goths are ever scheming and deceiving. They bribed the despicable Bastarnae to cause mischief on our northeastern borders - raiding cattle, killing the odd herdsman. Small things. To leave these acts unpunished would have been an invitation for the Bastarnae to invade. Apsikal selected a small force of seven hundred light cavalry. Unencumbered by the heavy cavalry they could travel fast. He left the heavy cavalry and the remaining Huns to protect the camp."

"Lucius, I have fought the Bastarnae numerous times. Their name means 'the people of the boar'. Like wild boar, they live in the forested region of the steppes. They fight with the spear and the bow and are strangers to the way of the horse. Like the Goths, they make their living by digging in the dirt."

"Yes, I remember you telling me about the Bastarnae long ago", I said. "They are not known to be great warriors and our people always thought of them as an irritation rather than a threat."

"Your memory serves you well", the king replied.

He drank again and continued. "Have you heard of the Heruli?"

"No, I have not", I said.

"Many generations ago, it is said, the forefathers of the Goths lived on the Ice Islands across the Northern Sea. The people who still live there is a race as hard as iron. Some of these Heruli have settled on the steppes, close to the navigable rivers where they keep their longships. From these bases, they raid and plunder far and wide. Some call them the 'people of the sea' and they are as at home on a ship as we are on a horse. These huge warriors believe that they are the chosen ones of their dark war god, Woden, who they invoke through magic markings on their bodies, weapons and armour."

"I tell you this, because the Goths had paid these mercenaries, the Heruli, to fight at their side", Bradakos said.

He remained quiet for a while and I could see that he struggled to relay what had happened. Bradakos swallowed hard and continued in a soft voice.

"Apsikal would not listen to me and he pursued the Bastarnae into the trees. It was in the forest that the Heruli warriors were waiting for us. Apsikal's horse died when a huge brute nearly severed its neck with his broad-bladed battle-axe. I rode next to the king and was also unhorsed in the confusion."

"A giant of a man with hair as white as snow came at me. He had the skin of a white bear draped over his shoulders, and his whole body down to his knees was protected by thick chain."

"Lucius, I did not know that a man could be that strong. He wielded a huge axe in one hand as if it had no weight at all. His hands are twice the size of mine."

"Bradakos, you are a noble warrior and I know that you do not exaggerate", I said.

He nodded and continued. "He struck my shield and it broke into three pieces. My left arm was numbed by the blow. I tried to parry the next blow with my sword and it bent. I lost my footing, slipped and fell in the mud. Just then, Apsikal ran to my side and pierced the calf of my enemy with his spear. The giant turned on him, grabbed his spear, and struck him on the chest with his axe, slicing through the scale armour and inflicting a mortal wound."

"I regained my footing, but an arrow struck me in the shoulder from behind. Our cavalry had regained some sense of order after the ambush and our arrows started to find targets."

"I saw a Heruli a few feet to my left go down with at least six arrows protruding from his chest. The giant pointed his axe at me, grinned, and retreated into the depths of the forest with the rest of the Bastarnae and the Heruli."

"I crawled over to where Apsikal was bleeding his lifeblood into the forest."

"I thrust my bent sword into the earth and Apsikal gripped the hilt."

"Apsikal's knuckles turned white around my sword as his body shook in the grips of death and he said: 'I wanted to die this way, Bradakos.' He coughed and blood stained his lips. He whispered: 'Just be a good king to my people.' Then he was gone."

Tears were flowing freely down the king's cheeks. "Eochar, I was supposed to protect him, yet he was the one who saved me?"

I have never been good with words, so I think that Arash helped me in that moment.

"Bradakos, Apsikal knew that his time was short in this world", I said. "You are young and you are the future of the Roxolani. You are a brave warrior and a wise leader. He knew that when he willingly gave his life for the future of his people."

Bradakos nodded, accepting the truth of my words. "We took a few captives and they told us about the Heruli. The man who killed Apsikal is the leader of their war band. His name is Hygelac the White."

Bradakos stood and removed his upper garment to expose an ugly scar on the back of his shoulder.

"And tell Cai that the ridiculous-looking yellow silk tunic he gave me saved my life", he said. "The arrowhead only went in half an inch. Without the tunic, I would have been dead."

Chapter 18 – Thervingi

Bradakos was adamant to send three hundred riders to escort me to the lands of the Thervingi Goths.

I refused. I was unwilling to risk the lives of three hundred of my people. We nearly came to blows, but in the end Bradakos relented.

We settled on him providing us with three of the Huns' best scouts and two Hunnic horses for each of us.

Once we had agreed, I left to join Marcus and Cai. I wished to wash in the river and rest before we would attend the compulsory feast in our honour. Barbarians know how to feast and I expected that the king would lay on something proper.

Earlier, while I met with Bradakos, Cai and Marcus had enjoyed a swim in the river. After I, too, washed off the sweat and grime from the journey, I joined my friends in our tent.

Typical of Cai, he was not forthcoming with information, but Marcus was keen to be updated.

Marcus ambushed me as soon as I entered our tent.

"Lucius, tell me what happened. How is it possible that you can get an audience with a barbarian king? Why are they treating us like royalty?"

I sighed on the inside, knowing that I had to take the direct and honest route.

I drew my gladius, and for a heartbeat I noticed a bit of worry in Marcus's eye.

I grinned at that and said: "Don't be concerned Marcus. I would have done it already if I wanted to."

He chuckled, and replied sheepishly: "I know Lucius, it's just when you draw your sword, people normally start dying."

"I will tell you as much of the truth as I can", I said. "But only if you make an oath on this blade never to reveal it."

He immediately placed his hand on the sword and said: "I will not share anything. On the honour of my family name."

I told Marcus everything that he needed to know.

I explained to him that my mother was a Roxolani princess and that I would have been the king of my people. I told him about the Huns and the battle with the Goths.

Needless to say, I left out the part where my father killed the emperor.

After I had finished my story, Marcus just sat there for a while with his mouth slightly ajar.

When he had gathered his wits he said: "Lucius, had I not known you, I would have thought that you have a talent for telling tall tales. Thank you for sharing this with me."

He had barely finished speaking when one of the king's bodyguards came to fetch us for the feast.

Marcus muttered something about being tired, but I told him: "Marcus, there is no choice here. The king will be hugely insulted should you not accept his invitation. Even I would not be able to prevent them sacrificing you to appease some dark god."

My ruse worked. Marcus suddenly felt less tired and decided to join us.

A small crowd awaited us. I was escorted to the seat of honour, on the right side of the king, with Cai and Marcus occupying the seats reserved for important guests.

It was truly a fine evening and the wine and food was delicious. I eventually had to drag Marcus home, who seemed to have taken to the barbarian ways.

The sun had not risen yet when we broke our fast on leftover meat from the previous evening. We donned our Roman garb and awaited the arrival of the Hun scouts.

I had made quite an impression on the war band of my Hun friend, Gordas. When the scouts arrived, they bowed their heads and reported.

"Lord Eochar, the favourite of Arash, we are honoured to serve you." I greeted them in their own language. I turned to Marcus and said: "Please do not stare at them my friend, they interpret staring as a challenge to mortal combat."

That ended the staring thing. No one relishes single combat with a Hun.

In any event, we left camp mid-morning. Elmanos and his warriors were given the task of escorting us to the borderlands. This was seen as a great honour.

Marcus initially scowled when we had to relinquish our Roman horses for the smaller Hun horses.

"Marcus, if we need to escape capture, no other horses in the world will be able to catch us. A Hun horse will outlast and outrun anything. Trust me, they might save your life."

He accepted my wisdom, but I must admit that we appeared far less regal on our small mounts.

We rode north and then east for five days, relaxed in the company of our Roxolani hosts, the Hun scouts ranging far ahead. In the evenings we feasted on some or other wild animal taken down by the warriors during the day. Bradakos had been generous, providing Elmanos with a stash of good wine for our enjoyment.

On the morning of the fifth day we came across a shallow river, the name of which I do not recall. Elmanos rode up to me and said: "This is the border of the Roxolani tribal lands. The king told me that I may accompany you if you can be persuaded?"

"No, Elmanos, I cannot be persuaded", I said.

He grinned and said: "The king knows you well, lord."

I clasped his arm and he left us to cross the river, the Roxolani war band milling around on the bank until we were out of sight.

Marcus turned to me. "I thought the Huns would be scouting for us?" he said. "They are nowhere to be seen."

"Do not fear, Marcus", I said. "They are out there. From here on they will not show themselves, but they will be there. They will alert us should any enemy be close."

He nodded although he looked unconvinced, muttering something about barbarians not being trustworthy.

On the second day we left the Sea of Grass behind and rode through scrubland, which slowly gave way to the forested steppes. I knew where to go, as Bradakos had told me where I would find the main fort of the Thervingi. Like Rome, barbarians also had their spies.

We had not seen our Hun scouts for nearly three days when one of them appeared behind us from the gloom of the forest.

He held up his open palm as a sign for us to stop, and walked his horse past us. Without looking over his shoulder, he motioned for us to follow him.

We walked the horses down a rocky forested slope, crossed a small stream, and ascended again until we were level with the narrow trail we had been travelling on.

I nearly did not notice the other scout hidden behind a recently fallen oak.

We moved into the cover provided by the dead tree and all dismounted on the scout's instruction.

He put his finger to his lips, pointed to the trail, and gently placed his hand over the muzzle of his mount to stop any whinnying. We followed suit.

Heartbeats later a lone horseman appeared, slowly walking his horse along the trail. The warrior was clearly a scout. He sniffed the air and remained silent for at least a dozen heartbeats, taking in the sounds of the forest.

The man was tall and muscular with the skin of a wolf draped over his broad shoulders. He wore no helmet, but I noticed chain mail underneath his fur cloak.

The silence was broken by the distinct impact of an arrow, and next I saw an arrowhead protruding from the man's temple. He slumped in the saddle, but before he could topple from the horse, a hand stabilised the body and took the reins.

The head of the third Hun scout came into view as he slowly stroked the horse's head. As soon as the skittish animal had calmed down, he led it and its dead master towards our hiding place.

The Hun arrived shortly after, shrugged and said: "The scout sensed us. He had skill. I had to kill him when his hand went to his sword." I nodded in agreement.

The Hun pried the dead man's hand from the hilt of his sword. He drew it from the scabbard, revealing a magnificent blade, carved with strange writing symbols.

I realised that the scout was a Heruli mercenary, one of the feared wolf warriors from the Ice Islands of the north.

We became aware of a commotion caused by a multitude of men travelling along the trail. They were talking and laughing loudly, depending on their scout to warn them of any ambush.

We were not concerned that they would discover us as we were well concealed.

We counted at least one hundred and sixty men.

I was amazed at the size of them. Among any population, one tends to find the odd man who is larger and more muscular than the rest. Not so with the Heruli. They were all taller and more muscular than any warrior I had ever come across. Unlike the Goths, these men were all fully encased in armour and every man had a spear, as well as a sword or battle-axe.

In my heart I knew that they were on their way to the Goth settlement. The Goths had subjugated many smaller Scythian and Germanic tribes. Apart from the plunder, they also received an annual tribute in the form of grain, livestock, silver and gold.

They were cleverly using the excess funds to lure mercenaries to their cause. They had their sights set on the ultimate prize. The rich lands on the western banks of the Danube.

Although tempting, it was too risky to follow the war band. They would soon realise that their scout was missing and if they found us, the odds were not good.

We travelled at least five miles to the north and then resumed our course to the Gothic fort.

We must have wasted a day, or even two, but eventually our Huns found the settlement of the Thervingi.

Unsurprisingly, it was a hill fort, but much larger than I had expected. The fort was more or less square, protected by a wooden palisade on all four sides. Each of the sides of the palisade was at least half a mile long.

I could see guards with spears patrolling the walls. Bradakos had told me that the iudex of the Goths was called Argunt. The same ruler who had engineered the incursions into Pannonia.

My plan was simple. Marcus, Cai and I would just ride up to the gates of the fort and announce ourselves. I tried to come up with something better, but I could not. Neither could Marcus or the ever wise Cai.

I instructed our Hun scouts to remain hidden and wait for us for at least seven days.

Marcus and I groomed our horses, made sure our armour and clothes were spotless and walked our horses out of the forest to the gates of the Gothic town, with Cai trailing behind.

We slowly moved towards the open gates. Nobody noticed us at first. The only thing that set us apart from other travellers were our distinct Roman military garb.

A guard at the gate had the clarity of mind to call out an alarm, and soon we were surrounded by a dozen guards addressing us in some unintelligible Gothic dialect.

I spoke in Scythian like we had rehearsed. "We are ambassadors from the great King of the West, come to pay homage to the King of the Goths."

The captain of the guard stared at us blankly, but one of his subordinates walked up to him and spoke to him in a low voice. I assumed he understood some Scythian.

We were taken inside the fort, and the captain of the guard gestured for us to wait. Within a sixth of a watch, a man arrived. His hair and beard was nearly white with age, but his bearing was that of a noble. He was dressed in rich furs, and a longsword hung from his belt.

The man spoke to us in passable Scythian. "My name is Hildebald, Erilaz of the Thervingi. What is your business in the lands of the Goths?"

As Marcus was unable to understand or speak a word of Scythian, I answered.

"Earl, I am called Lucius, and this man is Lord Marcus." I did not mention the name of Cai, as he was a servant and not worth a mention.

"We are ambassadors of the Roman Emperor, come to deliver a message to the iudex of the Thervingi", I added.

I inclined my head as a sign of respect.

"You are welcome to our land, Romans. I offer you my hospitality", the Goth replied.

Hospitality is not only a word in the land of the Germanic tribes. When you are offered hospitality, it means that your safety is ensured and that you have the right to be granted any reasonable request. The reverse is also true, so that, should you accept hospitality, a reasonable request put to you may not be refused.

We followed Earl Hildebald to his home. His home, or rather compound, was enormous.

There were three large buildings made from wooden logs. His oathsworn warriors lounged around one of the halls, which was clearly where they resided. Some were engaged in talk while others trained with swords and spears.

"Your servant will stay in the stables with your horses", Hildebald said, and pointed to one of the large buildings. He exchanged some words with a servant, who led Cai away with the horses in tow.

We walked to the great hall of the earl.

In the dim light of the interior, a woman of the same age as Hildebald, walked towards us. She fell in next to Hildebald. "This is my wife, Avagisa", he said.

Marcus and I both inclined our heads as Hildebald introduced us to his wife.

Avagisa looked at me and replied in perfect Scythian: "I was the one who taught Hildebald Scythian. I am from the Greuthungi of the northern steppes."

She looked at me curiously. "How come a Roman officer speaks fluent Scythian?" she asked.

"My mother was of the Roxolani, Lady", I replied.

I noticed that Hildebald flinched when I mentioned the name of my people. Avagisa was a perceptive woman. She winked at me. "Do not be concerned about my husband's reaction, they have had little success in their effort to bring the Roxolani to heel."

Contrary to my expectations, I immediately warmed to Hildebald and Avagisa, who made me feel at home.

I turned to Marcus and related the conversation to him.

Marcus shrugged and said: "We have no decision-making power, we are only messengers. I expected to be killed on sight. This looks to be a much better alternative. Let's just relax and enjoy our time here."

"I have sent a message to the iudex", our host said. "When we are summoned, I will accompany you."

"Unlike me, my brother Argunt is a very suspicious man", he added.

Chapter 19 – Kniva

Hildebald had hardly finished speaking when someone burst into the hall.

A girl, maybe three or four years my junior, walked briskly towards the earl and embraced him.

"Thank you, Father, the horse is magnificent!" she exclaimed.

She was tall for a woman, with white blonde hair. What drew my attention was her eyes, which nearly matched her hair.

She turned to me, said something in her language, and smiled.

All I could do was to smile back like the idiot I was.

Her mother came to my rescue and said in Scythian: "These men are from the lands of the Romans, Segelinde. They are emissaries come to see your uncle. Your father has extended hospitality to them and they will be staying with us. This here is Lucius and the other is Lord Marcus."

I was so focused on Segelinde that I did not see the young man who appeared on the other side of the earl. He spoke and it made me jump, only to appear a greater fool in front of the beautiful girl.

Like his sister and mother, he spoke Scythian and said: "I am Cannabaudes, but please call me Kniva."

I could not help but notice that he shared his sister's good looks, with a fierce intelligence emanating from his blue eyes.

I decided to match his spontaneity and replied: "I am Lucius, but you may call me Eochar."

Marcus tapped me on the back, bringing me back from the spell, and I quickly added: "And this is Lord Marcus."

We were shown to our quarters, a room within the hall, separated from the rest by wooden panelling.

Cai delivered our baggage to the room, which included our weapons.

"I am sorry that you have to sleep in the stables, Cai", I said.

"Horse better company than Goth", he replied and winked at me.

Cai never did mind to play the willing servant, and although I felt a bit bad about it, he did volunteer. It also placed him in a position to scout the area without drawing too much attention to himself.

Later that afternoon Segelinde invited us to share drinks with the family.

She poured each of the men a horn of an unidentifiable substance, which smelled like mead. As I had a less than pleasant experience with mead years ago, I was reluctant at first. Segelinde explained that it is a brew made only for special occasions. It contained barley, honey, meadowsweet and mint. Just to be on the safe side, I drank sparingly.

I was not accustomed to the presence of women when it came to family gatherings, so it was the closest I have ever come to a real family feast. Although I tried not to show it, I was infatuated with Segelinde.

Throughout the evening I acted as interpreter between Marcus and the others. Our hosts were extremely curious about the Romans. All they knew was that the Romans are a warlike people who lived to the west, beyond the great river. They understood that the Romans, not unlike the Goths, had subjugated many tribes and races and had incorporated them into their empire. It was also told that the Roman lands contained unimaginable treasure and wealth, available to the warriors strong enough to conquer its countless legions.

We tried to be as honest as possible in our answers, obviously refusing to answer any question that could be seen as giving away military secrets. Our hosts were respectful and understanding.

I never imagined that I would feel so comfortable among the Goths. I did not forget that they were my sworn enemies, and although I liked the family, I was destined to face the Goths on the field of battle.

As was our habit, Marcus and I awoke before sunrise the following morning. We soon realised that we were the only ones awake. The last thing we wanted to do was to wake our hosts prematurely. We stayed in the room in hushed conversation for what felt like a watch.

The sun was already high when servants carried in two wooden baths. Soon they had them filled with hot water.

Romans believe that barbarians are filthy savages. That is far from the truth.

We enjoyed the bath, afterwards drying ourselves with the pieces of linen provided. The servants had added herbs to the bath water which left us smelling good and feeling refreshed.

The smell of grilled smoked pork filled the hall as we emerged in our clean tunics.

The food was placed on a table close to the hearth fire. I was confronted with another difference in culture. Rather than the family taking their food together, seated around a single table, each person took the food that was to his liking and sat apart.

Kniva was putting an edge to his sword while Segelinde was stitching a garment, intermittently picking at the meat in her bowl.

Hildebald sat at a small table, eating and already enjoying some of the brew we shared the previous evening.

Before we could object, a servant handed each of us a sizeable horn filled with the same brew. It did go down well with the fatty meat and rich cheese that accompanied the meal.

While we were enjoying the meal, a messenger arrived for Hildebald.

Once everyone had finished eating, Hildebald walked over to us and said: "I have had word from Argunt, or rather, from his household. The Costobocci on our eastern borders have been causing mischief and the iudex has travelled there to address the problem. They could not tell me when he would be back."

"Do not be concerned", he added. "You are welcome to our hospitality until the king returns."

Segelinde was sitting within earshot and I could see her smiling at the news.

"Father, why do we not go hunting today?" Kniva suggested. "I am sure our guests would enjoy it."

The earl allowed Marcus and me to use two of his horses. I was surprised at the quality of the animals.

Hildebald walked up to me while I was stroking the flanks of the gelding. "It is not good that you ride around on the horses used by our mortal enemies", he said. "People will talk and it will reach the ear of the king."

He did not look at me and I did not reply. What could I say?

I took my Hunnic bow, unstrung within its leather holder. My jian sword was strapped to my saddle. Kniva handed me a boar spear.

Marcus took only his sword. He was given a spear as well.

The forest that we rode through teemed with game.

Kniva must have noticed my surprise. "This part of the forest is reserved for the nobility", he explained.

As we rode deeper into the forest the canopy became denser, and it was as if it had become early dusk. One of the oathsworn that accompanied us rode thirty paces in front. He held up his hand and all of us came to a stop.

I heard the unmistakeable squealing of juvenile wild boar. Kniva dismounted.

Thirty paces to my left a huge sow appeared, sniffing the air.

Kniva did not hesitate. He took a step towards the animal and cast his spear. If I had not witnessed it, I would have thought it impossible to launch a spear with such force. The heavy spear struck the sow like a thunderbolt. It went straight through the thick ribcage, slicing through the heart and vital organs.

I was still in awe of what I saw when a massive boar burst from the undergrowth close to where the sow lay.

Kniva proved to me that his first feat was not by chance. He calmly launched a second spear at the enormous animal that was running at full speed.

The spear hit the animal so hard that its legs buckled. It skidded through the dead leaves, coming to a rest about ten paces away. Marcus and I were ready to save Kniva should the animal rise again, but the throw had been so powerful that the animal was killed instantly.

I had always been proud of my martial prowess and it was a rude awakening for me to realise that there may actually be men that possessed more skill or talent.

Marcus was still staring at me, wide-eyed, when I turned to a grinning Kniva. "Kniva, I have never seen anyone yield a spear the way you did just now."

His father replied from ten paces away. "That is why I never hunt with him anymore. I never get a chance to kill anything." He pointed with his spear to the dead boar. "That is how they all arrive."

At least we did not go home empty-handed. Both Marcus and I ended up spearing a small boar from horseback, although it was nothing as impressive as Kniva's feats.

We did not hunt again, but we spent the following couple of days riding with Kniva and Segelinde.

We explored the forest and inspected the cattle herds of the earl, or just rode to view interesting landmarks. At least four of Hildebald's oathsworn accompanied us every time. They were hard men. I counted the scars on their forearms and faces. I am sure that I could have dealt with them without breaking a sweat, should I had wanted to, but I did nothing to suggest that I possessed such skills.

Chapter 20 – Feast

A messenger arrived and informed Hildebald of the return of his brother, the iudex.

Argunt allowed us to stew for three days before granting us an audience.

During that time we learned that he had dealt the Costobocci a crushing defeat. It might not have been a war, but it was a major skirmish at the least.

The victorious army consisted of five hundred Goths and five hundred Heruli. No prisoners were taken. The Costobocci had apparently laid down their arms but the Heruli slaughtered them to the last man.

Allow me to digress. Only a Goth is allowed be king of the Thervingi.

The Goth warriors will only follow a brave ruler who leads from the front. Argunt, like his brother Hildebald, was past his prime. The king had no children.

All this I gained from my conversations with Segelinde and Kniva. It played a major role in the events that were about to unfold.

Hildebald accompanied Marcus and me to the hall of the king.

We left our weapons at the home of our host and the king's guards ushered us inside after searching us for concealed weapons.

Argunt was a powerful, muscular man. Like Hildebald, his beard and hair was grey.

The king was seated on an elevated chair. To his right stood a monster of a man. His broad shoulders were covered with the skin of a white bear, his braided hair matching the hair of the animal. His chain mail extended to his knees, with his lower legs protected by bronze greaves.

Strange tattoos were etched between the white scars on his forearms and his left cheek. They were the magic writings of the Heruli, the masters of the runes.

All in our group went down on one knee. The king did not give us permission to rise.

Marcus held the leather tube containing the scrolls in his hand and offered it to the king. A servant took it and handed it to the king who inspected the seal and nodded.

He opened the tube and took out the scroll. The message was written in both Latin and Greek.

The king called out a name, and a man appeared from the back of the tent. Argunt handed him the scroll and he read the content in silence. I assumed that the man was a Greek.

He approached Argunt, and in a low whisper related the content to the king, who appeared pleased.

The iudex smiled and said something to Hildebald, which none of us could understand. Hildebald turned to me and said in Scythian: "King Argunt accepts to meet with your emperor. He will compose a message for you to take back to your master."

Argunt dismissed us with a wave of his hand. We bowed low and backed out of the hall.

When we were outside Marcus said to me: "That was easier than I expected. I initially thought that this was a suicide mission but it turned out to be more like a holiday."

"Do not tempt fate, my friend", I said. "But I do tend to agree with you."

During the afternoon we were all summoned to attend a feast that same evening. Hildebald and his whole family were to join us.

Marcus and I dressed in our official military garb. Marcus's bronze and black muscled cuirass and plumed helmet made my centurion's uniform look bland in comparison. Hildebald and Kniva both wore brown woollen leggings with richly embroidered tunics and soft brown leather boots. Both were draped in thick green woollen cloaks fastened with large silver brooches.

Avagisa and Segelinde wore blue cotton dresses. Their cloaks matched those of the men, but their brooches were studded with a variety of precious gemstones.

I struggled to keep my eyes off Segelinde, worried that all would notice.

Hildebald lived close to the hall of the king and at the appointed time we left, escorted by his oathsworn. The Gothic warriors walked at the front of our retinue, clearing the streets for their earl.

The feast was not an intimate family affair.

There were at least a hundred people in attendance. I did not mind, as Marcus and I were seated opposite Segelinde and Kniva. Hildebald and Avagisa sat with the important elders.

Slaves brought platters of meat - mutton, boar, deer and pork.

Unlike a Roman affair, the guests were laughing and shouting out loud. Not that different from a Roxolani or a Hun feast.

Ale and mead were freely available, but I tried not to overindulge, unlike the majority of the guests.

Hygelac the White occupied the seat of honour to the right of the king. I learned during the course of the evening that the main reason for the feast was to celebrate the victory over the Costobocci.

When Kniva left to speak with friends, Segelinde shared her concerns with me.

"Eochar, I fear for the future and the safety of our family. Ever since Argunt had allowed the Heruli into our midst, it became evident that the white-haired pig covets the throne. The king has no heir. Kniva has the strongest claim to the throne next in line to Argunt, but the pig is poisoning the king's mind against my brother. I fear that soon Hygelac will make an attempt on Kniva's life."

She drank from her horn of ale and continued. "But he will strike from behind. Kniva is already a formidable warrior and few will be able to defeat him in combat."

I had no wise words or solution ready. "What does Kniva have to say about this?" I asked.

She sighed and said: "Kniva is only interested in being a warrior. He trains every single waking moment. He does not covet the throne."

I looked away and smiled, thinking about how similar we were. I looked up again, into angry blue eyes. A frown creased her brow.

I laughed. "I am sorry. Segelinde, he is just so similar to someone I know."

She smiled, and said: "You men. You are insufferable."

While Marcus spoke to me I noticed Segelinde leave the table. Accompanying her outside was a girl of a similar age.

After a while Marcus engaged in some drunken conversation with the girl who sat next to him and I decided to seek some fresh air as well. Kniva followed me outside.

"I needed an excuse to leave those men, they drink too much", Kniva said with slightly slurred speech.

It took some time for our eyes to become accustomed to the near dark.

Kniva was saying something when we heard a scream. A distinctive female scream, originating from around the corner of the wooden hall.

Kniva and I shared a look and ran towards the sound. I saw Segelinde fall onto her back in the mud and Hygelac the White towering over her in a menacing way.

It was clear that Hygelac had either pushed or struck Segelinde, and in that moment I feared for her life. I ran and bent down next to her, completely ignoring the huge Heruli. I noticed that she was bruised, but alive. I turned towards

Hygelac, but halfway through the turn his enormous boot struck the base of my skull and the world went black.

Chapter 21 – Laws of hospitality

I woke with the familiar face of Cai studying me.

"If I not look after you, these things happen", he said.

I wanted to protest, but I was still too drugged from whatever Cai had forced down my throat.

Heartbeats later he produced a mug with one of his potions and said: "Drink."

It tasted disgusting but I knew better than to argue with Cai.

When I woke again, it was morning, and Segelinde and Kniva were both sitting next to my bed. Marcus leaned against the wall, a few paces away. I glanced around nervously, just to make sure that Cai was not waiting in ambush.

"Don't worry, Eochar", Kniva said, "your servant is not here with a potion. He said that you would be back to normal today and that there is no need to babysit you."

Kniva frowned and added: "By the way, you are too lenient with that servant, Eochar. He has no respect."

I ignored his rebuke and said: "Tell me what happened."

Kniva looked at Segelinde and she related the events.

"I went outside with my friend Romilde for some fresh air. Romilde is the girl your friend Marcus had been eyeing the whole evening", Segelinde said.

Hearing his name in the same sentence as Romilde's, Marcus just nodded and grinned like an idiot.

"We were talking about things when Hygelac approached", she added.

"Eochar, the things they were talking about were you and Marcus", Kniva said, grinning.

Segelinde hit Kniva in his chest with the back of her hand and blushed. "I asked Hygelac to leave, as we did not desire his company."

"I've always been the sibling with tact", Kniva added.

She frowned at him and said: "I am not someone for mincing my words. At least people know where they stand with me without having to guess."

"Hygelac put his arm around me and said that he would speak with my father about me being his bride", Segelinde said. "I kneed him in the groin. When he recovered, he menacingly approached, grinning. He slapped me with the back of his open hand and I fell. That was the moment you and Kniva arrived."

"He kicked you when you attempted to tend to me. When Hygelac stepped forward to kick you again, my brother hit him on his temple. Kniva hit him so hard, I think a normal man would have died, but the giant Hygelac only stumbled backwards."

"The Heruli smiled then, and in that moment I was sure that he had orchestrated everything to achieve his goal. He spat into the mud, showing his contempt, and said: 'I challenge you, boy. You have insulted my honour. We will do this the old way.' He walked away with a spring in his step."

"Hygelac is a Heruli, an elite warrior, but he is also kin of the Goth", Kniva explained. "He desires the throne and he thinks that eliminating me will bring him one step closer."

"And he is correct", Segelinde said. "With Kniva out of the way, he would then focus on getting rid of my uncle."

I sat upright in the bed and looked around the room.

I saw no sign of Hildebald, but Avagisa was stitching, looking generally distraught.

"He has gone to speak with Argunt", Kniva said. "My father is adamant that Hygelac withdraw the challenge."

Just then Hildebald entered the hall. His face was dark and brooding. He shook his head and looked at Avagisa, who appeared even more distraught. His attempt to get the duel set aside had obviously failed.

Looking back, I always wonder how different the world could have been if I had not acted the way I did. I believe that there are only a few times during a man's life where his actions or decisions alter the course of his life and even the course of history. I am also convinced that those decisions are guided by the hands of the gods.

This was one of those opportunities.

I rose from the bed feeling absolutely fine, and gestured for Kniva to follow me. I walked over to Hildebald, inclined my head and said: "Earl, I wish to discuss an issue with you and your son."

Hildebald called for mead, and we sat down next to the hearth fire in the centre of the hall.

Even though the women would be able to hear parts of the conversation, they would not interrupt.

I took a deep breath. "As I have told you, my mother was a Roxolani. What I did not tell you is that she was the sister of the king. King Apsikal of the Roxolani was my uncle."

Hildebald nodded and said: "You were honest with us, but had enough cunning not to tell all. Cunning is a virtue of a warrior."

Relieved, I continued: "There is more."

I heard Arash whisper a plan into my ear and I replied: "My uncle was killed by Hygelac the White. I have taken an oath of vengeance. I noticed him at the king's side, but it would not have been honourable for me to fight him while you have granted me hospitality."

Again Hildebald nodded and said: "Should you have challenged Hygelac, it would have brought great dishonour onto our home. You did good to act with restraint."

I was ready to play my trump card. "By kicking me in the face while I was attending to your daughter, Hygelac greatly insulted my honour", I said. "I also swore an oath of vengeance. Should Kniva kill him, he would forever rob me of my vengeance."

I saw that both father and son were thinking deeply about my words.

I drew a breath and continued: "I know that any reasonable request of a person enjoying hospitality must be granted. I beg of you to allow me to fight Hygelac to restore my honour, and provide me with the vengeance I have sworn."

I could see that I had given Hildebald a great deal to think about. Kniva appeared stunned.

"I would like to speak with my son before I give you an answer, Eochar", Hildebald replied. "This is not an easy decision."

I nodded and left them to deliberate the answer that would determine the destiny of a nation.

I went to find Cai, who was meditating in the stables. I waited until he was done and told him what had happened.

Cai nodded. "Kniva is wise, he use hand of enemy to catch snake."

I nodded, suddenly feeling foolish, and left to find Marcus.

I found him sparring with the earl's oathsworn. It was good-natured, so I sat down to watch.

Kniva joined me a while later and said: "You are a man of great honour and courage, Eochar. I left it to my father to make the decision. He is a wise man."

Later that afternoon Hildebald summoned Kniva and me to the hall.

He was in a serious mood. "I have considered your request, Eochar, and I have decided to grant it", he said. "It is not uncommon for a friend to take the place of another in the 'Holmgang', the trial by combat."

"In your case, you have a valid blood feud", he added, "but above all, you have made a request under the laws of hospitality. Your request is reasonable. I must grant it. But I have to ask first if you can handle a blade? I will not send you to a certain death, even though I am willing to grant your request."

I was never a boaster. "I have been given adequate instruction in sword fighting, Earl", I replied. "I am sure that you would not send me to my death."

He was not so easily convinced. "Show me", he said.

He gestured for me to follow him. Kniva followed us outside to where Marcus was training with the oathsworn.

Hildebald turned to me. "I will ask them to bring two blunted blades used for training", he said.

I nodded and waited.

The earl spoke to his men, and one left to summon the warrior the earl was seeking.

A few heartbeats later, a tall and sinewy warrior walked from the hall housing the oathsworn.

Hildebald spoke to him briefly, and handed him a blunted sword.

"I have asked him to test you", he said, and handed me a sword. "Second only to Kniva, Herwig is our best swordsman."

My greatest concern was hurting Herwig, as that might be an insult to the earl.

I inclined my head to the warrior as a sign of respect, and swung the longsword to test its balance. It was satisfactory, although inferior to my eastern sword.

Herwig attacked and I parried each strike with ease.

The earl scowled at me and said: "Eochar, convince me or I will not allow it."

I put Herwig on his backside five times in a row without hurting him.

Hildebald nodded and I clasped Herwig's arm, helping him up yet again.

"You have convinced me", he said, and walked back to his hall.

Kniva slapped me on the back. "You are much better than I thought, Roman", he said. "But I think that you are still hiding your skill."

Chapter 22 – Holmgang (Trial by combat)

According to the ancient laws of the Goths, the Holmgang had to take place within seven days of the challenge, but not sooner than three.

Hildebald informed the king that I would take the place of Kniva in the trial by combat. The king agreed, having great regard for honour and the laws of hospitality.

Argunt proclaimed that it would take place two days hence, on the night of the full moon, to honour the goddess Mani, the sister of the sun god.

The atmosphere within the household of my host was tense during the time leading up to the trial.

Should I be killed in the duel, I would not be the only one to lose something. Hildebald brought the tiding that if Hygelac were victorious, he would be allowed to claim Segelinde as his bride. This was a request from the leader of the Heruli, and due to Segelinde's involvement in the dispute, the king deemed it a fair settlement.

On the upside, should I be victorious, Kniva could claim all the treasure owned by Hygelac. Even more important, there was a good chance that the Heruli warriors would give their oaths to Kniva as the party favoured by the gods.

The stakes were extremely high. Hildebald and Kniva spent most of their time outside, training with the oathsworn.

Avagisa and Segelinde cried frequently, causing Marcus and me to ride around aimlessly just to get away from the oppressive feeling of impending doom. We were however not allowed to ride around on our own without a couple of the hearth warriors protecting us. I was sure they were assigned to us to ensure I did not run away and leave Kniva high and dry.

Thankfully the big day soon arrived. We woke up late as usual. By now Marcus and I had given up our Roman ways.

The servants prepared a hearty breakfast, mostly consisting of generous portions of fried smoked pork and cheese. We even had honey, but to the surprise of our hosts I refused to drink any beer or mead.

Early afternoon I went in search of Cai in the stables.

"Cai, I need to be calm tonight", I said.

"Come, Lucius of the Da Qin, we meditate and breathe", he replied.

I joined Cai in breathing and meditation exercises and the time passed quickly. My mind was cleared of anxiety and fear, and I set off to find Hildebald and Kniva. I had items to negotiate before the big event.

The commoners of the tribe were not allowed to attend a Holmgang between nobles. As Kniva and Hygelac were both of high birth, attendance was by invitation only.

Five of the oathsworn of the Heruli accompanied Hygelac. The iudex and his two bodyguards were obviously in attendance. Marcus, Hildebald, his wife as well as Segelinde and Kniva attended the proceedings. In addition, five Gothic elders observed. As this was essentially a trial, their presence was required to add legitimacy to the duel, as well as to ensure that no foul play took place.

A duel was fought in a stone circle within the king's compound, and close to his hall. The circle was fifteen feet in diameter. The fight was to be to the death, but a combatant could step outside the circle, choosing life. The second option was seen by most as a worse fate than dying, as the contender would be branded a coward, and his spirit would never be accepted into the presence of the gods.

For once I left my Roman centurion's outfit in the hall of my host. Cai had wisely packed my Roxolani scale armour made from the hooves of horses. It was lighter than chain mail and more suited to single combat. I donned my standard Roman issue iron greaves worn by centurions. My forearms were protected by leather vambraces with strips of iron sewn onto the leather. I decided not to wear a helmet.

The Holmgang was traditionally fought with longswords. I was armed with my jian sword, a gift from Cai - the blade forged by a master swordsmith from the land of Serica. The weapon was strong, but extremely flexible and held an edge like none other.

As each combatant was afforded an assistant, naturally Kniva performed that role for me. Only the combatants were allowed to carry arms, but the assistant did carry additional weapons should both fighters agree to use alternative weapons in case of a stalemate.

Kniva and I approached the stone circle. It was well-lit by a multitude of torches placed on head high poles. Argunt and the elders sat on an elevated platform bordering the circle.

I studied my opponent who was standing at the opposite side of the circle. Hygelac was at least a head taller than me. His braided hair and beard was nearly white, but not due to age. He was born that way. He must have seen at least thirty summers. He wore a coat of mail that extended to his knees, with bronze greaves protecting his shins. On his enormous feet he wore undyed sealskin boots.

His left forearm and left cheek were tattooed with blue runes.

The sword he held was longer than any I had ever seen - it matched his build. I noticed that it had a longer than usual grip, indicating that it was designed as a two-handed weapon.

Hygelac was strong enough to yield it with one hand. His hand opened and closed on the hilt, and I could see the huge muscles flexing in his forearm.

He was studying me with intense blue eyes. It was clear that he was no dimwit. I had confidence in my abilities, but it was still intimidating to face such a large and powerful warrior.

The king held up his hand for silence and said something I did not understand.

"When the king drops his hand, the fight will commence", Kniva whispered.

Argunt lowered his hand. I drew my blade and stepped into the circle towards the advancing Hygelac who had also drawn his weapon.

I had expected him to attack immediately, which was normally the way of the Goths, but even though he towered over me, he was clever enough to first probe and find out what he was dealing with.

The way I had been taught to fight did not allow for my opponent to evaluate my swordsmanship. Once the opponent engages with me, I do not allow him to fall back and regroup.

The big man stepped forward with his left leg and executed a powerful thrust to my chest. It was a conservative move, not opening himself up, and difficult to parry.

Hygelac possessed enormous strength and it would have been folly to try and parry the move with only my sword. I gave a small step forward and slightly to the left, allowing his blade to scrape the scales of my armour while the flat of my sword slid against the edge of his blade, guiding it along its natural path.

He was too good a warrior to overextend with the first blow, and as he stepped back with his left foot, I stepped in, aiming a cut at his right leg. My unorthodox grip where the thumb reaches between the third and fourth finger, allows me extraordinary control over the jian, and as Hygelac parried my blow, I again met the edge of his blade with the flat of my sword.

My opponent was hovering close to the edge of the stone circle and suddenly his eyes darted to the side to try and establish how far he was from stepping over the line. It was a mistake.

I stepped back, allowing him the opportunity to attack.

Hygelac was visibly unsettled. I had been inside the danger area throughout the fight and had never given him a chance to gather himself. By then he must have realised that I possessed extraordinary skills. He was not a man who achieved his position in life by being overly cautious. He would attack as soon as I gave him half a chance.

I decided to give him a straw to grasp at, and retreated a step. In that moment I realised that he was going to gamble big. He stepped in to deliver a mighty horizontal cut, designed to take my head with a single blow.

My retreat was only a feint. I anticipated his move and lunged forward with my right leg, while keeping my left foot in position.

Cai had made me practise for endless hours. "Lucius of the Da Qin, power comes from hips, flows through spine and gathers momentum. The arm only there as path for energy to reach tip of blade."

I could feel the power surge through my hips into my spine, and at the last moment I let the sword deliver the energy as I executed a thrust at Hygelac's mailed chest. My lunge lowered the position of my body and Hygelac's mighty blade passed over my head harmlessly. The blow was delivered with such force, I doubt that a mortal man could have parried it.

I struck with speed and force. Hygelac had no chance.

My sword sliced through his mail like a hot dagger through cheese and entered his chest, piercing the giant's heart.

His knees buckled and he fell facedown in the dirt. I walked towards the corpse and took the scalp in the proven Hunnic way.

Two of Hygelac's warriors surged towards me, yelling something incomprehensible.

Kniva shouted a warning, but I was still kneeling next to the dead Heruli. As I righted myself I saw the warrior slicing down towards my exposed head with his sword.

Kniva's spear impacted with such force that it passed through mail and threw the warrior back at least three feet.

The second Heruli was only a step behind, but I was ready and easily dispatched him.

I felled the third of Hygelac's hearth warriors, but by that time the king's bodyguards had stepped in and restrained the remaining two Heruli.

The king stood facing the Heruli and said something in his language.

I heard Kniva's voice from close by. "The king said that they have no honour and there will be a price. It will have to be paid in blood."

Then Argunt turned towards Kniva and me, and spoke.

Kniva translated his words. "The gods have spoken. The Roman is the victor and you, Kniva, are legally awarded all of the treasure of Hygelac. His treasure is still under my control and I will ensure that you receive it soon." The elders nodded, demonstrating their agreement with the words of the iudex.

The king walked into the circle and picked up the sword of Hygelac and presented it to Kniva. He said something to my friend and walked away.

"This is a famous sword, it is called 'Oathbringer'", Kniva said. "The legend is that it was forged by the dwarves for Teiwaz, the god of war, who gave it to the first war leader of the Goths in our homeland across the sea."

He handed me the blade - it was truly magnificent. Many runes were etched into the blade.

"The runes endow the weapon with powerful magic", Kniva explained. "With this I will demand the oaths of the Heruli."

I did not know it yet, but I have helped to create a king. The king that would be a thorn in the side of the Empire for decades. But let me not get ahead of myself.

We made our way to our host's hall with haste, where servants hurriedly filled our horns with ale and mead. The lady of the house arranged for haunches of cold meat and rounds of cheese to be brought out for an impromptu feast.

Marcus took a deep swallow from his horn and stuffed a large piece of cheese into his mouth. "Lucius, tonight you have outdone yourself. I watched the faces of the Heruli. They saw your demise as a formality, like swatting a troublesome fly."

"It is an insult to you to call it a fight", Marcus said, and grinned. "Maybe they think that all Romans fight like you and leave us alone, eh?"

He took a long swallow from his horn, emptying it, and continued. "It is the most impressive fight in a Holmgang that I have ever witnessed."

"And it is the only one you have ever witnessed", I said, and grinned.

Hildebald was already enjoying his second horn of ale. He walked over to me and slapped me on the back. "I remember hearing a tale a few years ago. A tale that a Gothic war leader, a reiks, told Argunt. He relayed the story of a duel between a Roxolani boy and the champion of the Goths."

"Argunt had the reiks executed for being foresworn and failing in his mission."

"It would be impossible for a mere boy to defeat our champion. The tale said that the boy was the incarnation of Teiwaz."

He drank but held my gaze.

"If I had not been present tonight, I would not have believed it", he said.

"Kniva is good with a sword, but he would not have been able to defeat the Heruli. Hygelac was a monster, as strong as three men. And he fought with the sword of Teiwaz."

He shook his head. "Were you the boy who defeated our champion?" Hildebald asked.

"He did not last as long as Hygelac", I said, and nodded.

"Thank you for saving the life of my son", Hildebald said. "I will honour our arrangement. I am never foresworn."

Chapter 23 – Spoils (July 237 AD)

Argunt offered to arrange safe passage for us across the lands of the Bastarnae. We could not accept his offer, as I had unfinished business with Bradakos. We settled on Kniva and ten of Hildebald's oathsworn to escort us to the lands of the Roxolani.

Hildebald's household feasted us again on the evening prior to our departure. It was more a private dinner than a feast. I was amazed at how at home I felt in the hall of my sworn enemies.

Early the following morning we enjoyed a breakfast with our hosts. Afterwards Marcus, Kniva and I exited the hall with our travel packs and found Cai and the oathsworn waiting for us at the stables.

Hildebald muttered something to Kniva, who turned to me and said: "It will be here soon."

He had barely finished speaking when four heavily laden packhorses appeared at the open gate of the compound.

Two of the horses were led away towards the hall and two joined our group.

Marcus raised his eyebrows in a questioning look.

"It is our share of Hygelac's treasure", I explained. "Argunt owed him twenty thousand gold coins. As Hygelac is not able to collect it in person, we agreed to accept sixteen thousand coins in a full and final settlement of the king's debt. I negotiated with Hildebald and Kniva prior to the duel. You and I will have to share eight thousand gold coins."

Marcus was stunned and clearly at a loss for words. He just stared at me and shook his head, grinning.

He was still in shock when Segelinde walked from the hall, followed by a female servant carrying a travel pack.

"I negotiated for an additional treasure that I will unfortunately not be able to share with you", I added.

He frowned, for a moment not understanding what I meant. Then he saw Segelinde and her servant both mount, and his frown turned into a grin.

"Your negotiating skills far surmount your fighting skills, brother", Marcus said.

We both mounted and our little convoy walked the horses through the gate.

Chapter 24 – Princess

We were still within the territory of the Thervingi Goths, and the warriors escorting us seemed relaxed. We slowly made our way along the paths that traversed the forested landscape.

Although the pace was easy, we nonetheless called a halt at midday to allow the horses to rest.

Marcus and I were chatting to Kniva and his sister when the Gothic warriors suddenly started to yell and mount their horses.

Fifty paces ahead of us I noticed two Hunnic scouts inspecting us from the backs of their horses.

Kniva had drawn his sword and was running for his horse. "Please calm the warriors, Kniva", I shouted. "These men are here to protect us."

Moments later Kniva and his oathsworn were bunched together, a couple of paces behind me.

Kniva looked at me sceptically. "You surely cannot trust these savages, Eochar", he warned. "I would not turn my back on them if I were you. They will put an arrow in it."

I scowled at the Goths, turned around, and walked towards the Huns.

"Get off the horses and put away your bows", I told the Hunnic scouts. "And for the sake of Arash, come meet these people."

They were extremely reluctant, but they knew better than to gainsay the favourite of the war god. They slowly walked towards us, leading their mounts.

I turned towards the Huns. "I am in your debt for waiting for us", I said. "You will be rewarded when we arrive at the camp of the Roxolani. I need you to scout and ensure that we are not surprised by an enemy."

They bowed low. "We are here to serve you, lord", the leader said.

I handed a leather satchel to one of the scouts. "Please take care of this for me."

He looked inside and smiled, clearly pleased. "It will be an honour, lord", he replied.

The scouts walked away and melted into the forest.

"What did you say to them?" Kniva asked with suspicion.

"I told them to leave you alone. Your scalps are mine", I said, and grinned.

Kniva was still scowling as I walked away to mount my horse and continue our journey.

Segelinde rode next to me for a while and I explained to her how I came to know the Huns so well. She was not impressed when I told her how I helped defeat a Gothic army, but she understood the happenings in light of the Gothic war leader breaking the blood oath.

The rest of the journey passed uneventful.

We travelled through the lands of the Goths. No one would dare attack Kniva and his retinue, who were clearly Gothic nobles.

We eventually reached the border of the Roxolani lands where Segelinde and Kniva shared a tearful goodbye.

I had negotiated for the hand of Segelinde. It was highly unusual, but as Hygelac would have won her as his bride, I could take his place as the victor of the Holmgang.

The fact that Segelinde was as keen on the marriage as I contributed to my success in persuading her family. The alternative for her was to eventually be married to some tribal chief twice her age. In the end it was not a difficult decision.

We were soon intercepted by a Roxolani border patrol led by a smiling Elmanos. This time there were no hostilities as he was clearly keeping an eye out for our return.

He dismounted and bowed his head when we approached. "It is good to see you, Lord Eochar. I see you travel with a Gothic hostage", Elmanos said.

"This is my bride to be, Lady Segelinde, and her servant", I replied.

Elmanos blushed bright red and inclined his head. "It seems that I have developed a habit of offending you, lord. Please forgive me, Lady Segelinde."

Segelinde smiled disarmingly at Elmanos. "Lord Eochar speaks highly of you, Elmanos. It is good to meet you", she said.

She had clearly won Elmanos over for life, and he smiled like an idiot, now even redder in the face.

During the following few days we were escorted by the Roxolani warriors to the camp of the king. I was itching to tell Bradakos what had happened, but he was now the king and I had to adhere to the necessary decorum.

We hadn't been in camp long when we received an invitation to dine with the king that very evening.

As was my habit, I rode to the nearby river to swim and wash after the long journey. I requested that the servants prepare some heated water for Segelinde inside our tent.

Elmanos even arranged for two warriors to guard the entrance to our tent while Segelinde was alone.

A typical male, it had slipped my mind to explain my relationship with Cai to Segelinde. At the allotted time Segelinde and I strolled over to the king's spacious tent. We were ushered in by the guards and found Cai and Bradakos already deep in conversation.

I could see that it was strange for Segelinde to see my servant speaking with a king. It was too late to inform her. I made a mental note to explain to her later, when we return to our tent.

Segelinde and I bowed to Bradakos, who greeted us, and personally handed each of us a golden cup filled with dark red wine. True to his nature he had dismissed the waiting servants to afford us more privacy. Platters of sliced meat, wild fowl and cheese were already laid out on the low table next to the central hearth.

Bradakos sat down, scowled and said: "Cai refused to tell me anything about your journey. He said that it makes a good story and that you will tell it."

I winked at Cai. "First, I have a present for the king", I said.

I handed him the leather satchel containing the scalp of Hygelac the White.

The Hunnic scouts had cleaned and worked the gory trophy at my request.

Bradakos opened the bag and withdrew the scalp.

I could see that he immediately knew what he was holding in his hand. He turned to me, finding it difficult to form the words. "Eochar, you have restored my lost honour", Bradakos said. "Ask me anything. Anything. If it is in my power, I will give it to you."

I expected him to be pleased over the demise of Hygelac, but his response was overwhelming.

True to the culture of the barbarians, it was my turn to respond, and no one would interrupt until I had spoken.

I took a long, slow swallow of wine. I could not ask for nothing, as that would be a slap in the face of the king. I did not desire treasure as I already had enough gold to last me ten lifetimes.

Two swallows of wine later, I put down my beaker and said: "Bradakos, I see you as an older brother. Your opinion means more to me than anybody else's. I have decided to take Segelinde as my bride. She is a princess of the Thervingi, our sworn enemies. I ask that you accept her into the tribe of the Roxolani and adopt her as your daughter. We will live in

Roman lands, but I know that she would forever be under your protection should the need arise."

Bradakos did not respond immediately. He was not expected to.

At last the king took a deep breath. "Eochar, what you ask for is no small thing, but I know your intentions are good."

He stood, walked around the hearth, and raised Segelinde by the hand.

"Welcome to my home, Segelinde, daughter, princess of the Roxolani."

He embraced her, kissed her on both cheeks, and then they sat down again.

Just like that my bride to be became a princess of the Roxolani.

"It is done", Bradakos said. "I will inform the elders. Let us not dwell on it any longer. My debt of honour is paid."

We spent a long, pleasant evening in the presence of Bradakos. I told my tale in detail.

When I told him about the Holmgang, Bradakos just shook his head in resignation. "Eochar, your duels never make good tales. It is over too quickly. Even if you are unable to let the fight last longer, I recommend you learn the skill of making the tale about the fight last longer."

When he had heard all, the king said: "I can see that my new daughter comes from a family who values honour. I support your choice, Eochar."

Although Bradakos requested that we stay longer, we reluctantly had to be on our way the following day.

I was still a soldier and realised that it would spell trouble should I arrive back in camp with a Gothic princess. We decided that Segelinde and Cai would travel with an escort of Roxolani and cross the river close to Sirmium. From there Cai and my bride would travel to my estate. I was not surprised when I found out that Elmanos volunteered to lead the escorting party.

Marcus and I would keep a low profile and travel with the Hunnic scouts on our way to report to the emperor who was still in Noviodunum.

On the day we left, Bradakos came to see us off and in turn embraced each of us, except Marcus, who he clasped arms with.

He took me aside.

"Eochar, I was greatly concerned about the reaction of the tribal elders to my adoption of Segelinde, mainly due to her being a Goth. Surprisingly, they embraced it, especially after they heard that my now future son-in-law had avenged the death of Apsikal. I had great difficulty calming them after I told them that my daughter would marry you in Roman lands, rather than here in the camp of the Roxolani."

I had said my goodbyes to Segelinde and Cai earlier, and I clasped forearms with Bradakos.

Marcus and I rode on our own, the Hunnic scouts ranging far ahead to keep us safe. I had rewarded each of them with twenty pieces of gold, therefore they were eager to please.

On the fifth day we reached the Danube. A Roman barge was anchored fifty paces offshore, and it was easy to draw their attention.

Two-thirds of a watch later we were back in camp.

I accompanied Marcus to the Praetorium, where we were immediately ushered into the presence of the emperor.

Maximinus Thrax was standing next to his desk, a large goblet of red wine in his hand. He seemed to be relaxed and was studying a document.

At the table, also enjoying a goblet of wine, a handsome young man was seated. He did not rise or even look in our direction.

The soldier emperor looked up and said: "Tribune, Centurion, I am delighted to see you back in camp."

Marcus and I went down on one knee, but the emperor dismissed it with a wave of his hand.

"I will have none of that. We are all soldiers here", he said.

Marcus handed him the scroll that he had received from Argunt, the iudex of the Thervingi.

The emperor handed it to his personal secretary, Aspasius, who unrolled it and immediately translated the Greek, whispering the words to the emperor.

"I am pleased. You have done well and will be rewarded", the emperor said.

He clasped arms with both of us and we were dismissed.

We walked out of the tent and Marcus asked: "Do you know what the scroll said?"

"Yes, Marcus, Kniva told me. He said that Argunt agreed to meet with the emperor on the day of the new moon. Which is only ten days from now."

"Argunt is looking forward to becoming an ally of the emperor", I added.

Marcus scoffed at my words. "I bet he is looking forward to the chests of gold he will be receiving", he said. "The Goths are growing in power. They have to be destroyed before it is too late."

"I agree, Marcus. But I sense that the emperor is cautious. He has many enemies in Rome and the senate despises his barbarian heritage. Should he campaign against the Goths, his empire might be usurped in his absence. He views the senate as a more dangerous enemy than the Goths."

"I tend to agree with him", Marcus replied after a while of silence. "The most immediate threat is from within."

Chapter 25 – Discontent

My first duty, after reporting to the emperor, was to announce my return to Hostilius.

I arrived at his quarters where his secretary waved me through without even looking up from the document he was reading.

Hostilius was seated behind his desk, sipping on watered wine while studying the writing on a wax tablet. A deep frown creased his forehead and from previous experience I knew that he was frustrated.

I saluted and announced myself.

"At ease Domitius", he said, "pour yourself some wine", and pointed to a flask and a cup upon a low table.

"I am not surprised to see you back in one piece. Did you have the pleasure of killing many of the Goth bastards?" he queried.

"Only one, Primus Pilus, but he was as big as two men", I said, and grinned.

Hostilius stood and clasped my arm. "It is good to have you back, centurion. I need all the good officers I can get with things being as they are."

It was my turn to frown.

"Being as they are?" I asked.

He slumped into his chair, sighed wearily, and gestured for me to take a seat.

"Centurion, let me tell you a story", he said.

"Three years ago a coalition of German and Scythian tribes crossed the Rhine, breached our border defences and sacked Roman lands. Severus Alexander, the previous emperor, assembled a massive army to drive the bastards out of our territory. The army consisted of eight legions and we managed to drive the barbarians back across the limes. They escaped with all their plunder because we never fought a pitched battle. A few minor skirmishes but nothing major."

"Severus was no soldier, but he was the emperor and we endured him. Many of the men lost family when the barbarians engaged in their killing spree. The legionaries were hungry for blood and revenge. Their purses would be filled by the spoils of war."

"Then Severus decided to rather pay off the barbarians."

"His generals tried in vain to persuade him to pursue the bastards across the river, like we all wanted to. We knew that the only way to achieve lasting peace was to crush them once and for all. In the end, he valued his mother's advice more than that of the generals."

"It started with one or two voices of discontent. Men openly speaking out against the cowardice of the emperor. Severus had them crucified."

"Within days the discontent grew like a malignant tumour within the legion, and it reached a tipping point. The next evening, Severus and his mother were dead. Murdered by the men of the Twenty-Second Legion."

"They reasoned that they had to remove him, because his planned payoff of the Germani reeked of cowardice and incompetence. Of course, that is all bullshit. It is all about the coin and exacting revenge for his harshness."

"The soldiers are willing to endure the severity of emperors if their pockets are lined with gold and plunder. With empty pockets they soon find a reason to become discontent."

Hostilius paused to drink deeply from his cup.

"While you were away, the emperor crucified a soldier for spreading discontent."

"It all seems too familiar - the stares, the murmurs. Like a ghost within the camp, not easy to come to grips with and eradicate."

"It gives me the creeps, Domitius. Rome cannot afford a repeat of what happened three years ago."

"The situation is worsened by the pretty boy son of the emperor, strutting around as if he owns the place. Maximinus shows the necessary respect to his officers, but that little peacock wipes his arse on the likes of you and me."

Hostilius breathed deeply to calm himself. "Our job is to keep the men calm despite the issues", he said. "Your century respects you, and most owe their lives to you. And last but not least, they know you are a killer. Only a fool antagonises a killer."

I joined my century a short while later and immediately met with my optio, Didius Castus, who barely managed to hide his relief at my return.

I shared my concerns with him and enquired about the morale of the century.

There had been no specific issues or any breach of discipline, but he shared the concerns of Hostilius.

It was nearly dusk and I decided to join my old contubernium to gauge the mood in the camp.

I arranged some or other urgent duty for the rest of their tent party and joined Ursa, Silentus and Pumilio around the fire.

All of them came to attention when I arrived, but I waved it away. They walked over to me and clasped my arm in turn.

Pumilio was the first to speak.

"Did you kill 'em all, or did you leave some for us?"

"I'm sorry friends, I had to kill them all, but I did bring you gifts", I replied with a grin.

I passed them each a purse with ten gold coins. "It's a present from the Goths, make no mention of it."

I produced an amphorae of an excellent vintage of red, and Ursa filled four cups in a flash.

Ursa raised his cup, took a deep swallow and smacked his lips. "We sure missed you, Centurion Umbra", he said.

Silentus rolled his eyes but Pumilio replied in a serious tone: "We are glad to see you. Things aren't all good and proper as they should be."

He drank, leaned in close, and continued in a low whisper. "It's no secret that I'm not fond of the Thracian, but some men are spreadin' real bad rumours and stuff. They say that he is on the side of them barbarians, given the fact that his parents were barbarians. That's the real reason he's paying 'em off with our coin."

"And what do you think?" I asked.

"We think that you should get rid of the shit-stirrer before the Thracian has the century decimated. That's what we think", Ursa replied.

"If they get rid of the Thracian, we will just get another one who might be worse. I say we keep what we've got. At least this one's a soldier", Pumilio added.

Silentus nodded his agreement.

They gave me the name of the troublemaker without me asking.

I am not a man plagued by procrastination. On the contrary, I may be accused of acting without enough thought. Yet that evening I had no immediate answer to the problem.

I considered to just hand the name to Hostilius, but that would surely have resulted in another crucifixion, which would have helped the cause of the rebels.

I reclined on my bed and sipped some red wine, trusting that a solution would present itself.

I sorely missed the advice of my mentor, Cai, but his absence could not be helped.

I must have dozed off because I heard Cai telling me: "Use hand of enemy to catch snake."

I woke with a jolt and knew exactly what to do. It was only the middle watch of the night and I went back to sleep.

As Cai was not with me, I rose early the following morning to prepare breakfast. I chopped up some smoked pork and mixed it with onions before frying it in olive oil. I wolfed it down with the previous day's bread and cheese. Just to be on the safe side, I poured myself half a cup of the leftover wine and diluted it with water. Then I set off to find my accomplice, Hostilius.

The Primus Pilus listened to my plan without interrupting, his frown getting deeper, and a scowl appearing closer to the conclusion.

"Domitius, my answer to anybody else would simply be a 'no'", he sighed. "But by now I know you well enough to believe that you could actually succeed. Tell me what to do."

We went through the normal duties of the day and by late afternoon I made my way to the area outside the camp dedicated to weapons training. I wore no armour, but only a heavy cloak over my tunic as the evening chill was already in the air.

I sat on a stool under a wooden pergola constructed for the benefit of officers overseeing the training. Ten paces in front of me I had positioned a small, low table. Two items lay on top of it. A purse and a dagger.

I waited patiently, and soon a single legionary appeared, carrying a bundle of wooden swords over his shoulder.

He was from my century and I recognised him immediately as the soldier I had been waiting for.

I hailed him. "Come join me, Titinius."

Titinius looked around suspiciously and walked over in my direction. He dropped the bundle and came to a halt next to the low table and saluted.

"At ease, Titinius. I have been waiting for you", I said.

Again, he looked to the right and left and even turned his head around to make sure we were alone.

"Relax legionary, we are alone. I have a proposal for you", I said.

While I was speaking, I loosened my belt which held my gladius and my dagger and cast it into the dust a couple of paces distant.

"Titinius, I want you to make a choice", I said.

He reached out and emptied the contents of the purse into his hand. It contained twenty gold coins. A fortune for a legionary. He placed the coins back into the purse and tied it to his belt. He then reached out and picked up the wickedly sharp dagger.

Grinning, he advanced on me. I stood with my hands behind my back.

"Centurion, somehow you must have found out. I cannot say that I dislike you, but you have to die now that you know", he said.

"I have killed more men with a dagger than I care to remember", he added. "I know you are good with a sword, but empty-handed, no man can defeat me. Nothing personal, sir, but you have to die."

By the way he held the dagger I realized that he knew his business, but I have trained with the Huns, as well as with Cai, the warrior priest from Serica.

I waited with my right fist clenched behind my back. He came at me with a combination of stabs and cuts. At the last moment, I deflected his wrist, stepped in, and slammed the side of my fist against his temple.

I patiently waited for him to regain consciousness.

After a while he started to moan and sat up, again glancing to his left and right, as if searching for my hidden accomplice. He stood and inspected himself for injuries, but found none.

"Do you know what they call me, Titinius?" I asked.

He looked right and left again and said: "They call you Umbra, the Ghost. They say you can traverse the lands of the barbarians without being seen because you transform into a spirit."

I had placed the dagger and the purse back on the table and he stared at it, but did not move to touch either.

"Legionary, I will give you a choice. Take the dagger and you will die. If you choose the purse, you will work for me and be well paid."

"How do you know I will not take the purse and disappear?" he asked.

"You may well do that", I replied. "But I will find you and you will regret it. If you break our agreement I will seek you out, even if you sail to Hyperborea."

He nodded, convinced. "What do I have to do?" he asked.

I pointed to a chair and said: "Sit, and I will explain."

He picked up the purse and tied it to his belt. Again he picked up the dagger, this time by the blade, and handed it to me hilt first before taking his seat.

"Pay close attention Titinius, this is what I need you to do."

Chapter 26 – Meeting

At first, we heard only the rumours.

Bees had made a nest in the Praetorium and did not sting the emperor when he entered.

During a bad storm in the night, thunder could be heard, but no lightning could be seen.

The emperor dropped his mirror, but it did not shatter.

Thirteen birds were seen sitting on the tent of the emperor and they did not take flight when disturbed.

I sat in Hostilius's tent. He was staring at me, shaking his head. "The rumours of the omens have spread through the army like wildfire. The men are convinced that the gods are on the side of the emperor."

"Domitius, have you ever considered becoming a priest?" he asked. "Nothing about you will ever surprise me again. Even if you volunteered to read the entrails prior to the next battle, I would just accept it as one of your talents that I was unaware of."

He looked around and lowered his voice. "I received reports of the disappearance of three men in the cohorts earlier today. I assume it had cost you sixty gold pieces?"

I nodded and he handed me a folded piece of parchment. "Discharge with full honours for Titinius. I hope I never have to lay eyes on the bastard again. If the Thracian knew he worked for the senate, he would have been on a cross rather than receiving a discharge."

He shrugged. "Anyway, it seems like all is well for the time being."

Two days passed before we received word that the Gothic delegation had arrived on the northern bank of the Danube.

My plan was to keep a low profile and let the meeting come and go without being involved.

The emperor and his bodyguards met with the iudex and apparently all went well. Argunt, like Maximinus Thrax, was a barbarian and it did not come as a surprise to me when I heard that a deal had been made.

I breathed a sigh of relief, convinced that I had been able to sidestep any involvement. That was until Marcus arrived.

He wore his broad smile. "Get ready for the party of the year, Lucius", he said. "We have been invited to join the emperor in celebrating the peace treaty with the Thervingi Goths."

I later realised that he had made a factual error. We were actually guests of honour of the Thervingi. But it matters not.

We arrived at the Praetorium at the intended hour, kitted out in full uniform.

Cornelius Carbo, the veteran senior tribune of the legion, met us outside the tent. He explained that we would be riding at the back of the procession that would attend the feast, set up on the island in the Danube.

The emperor and his retinue entered the tent set up for the occasion. A servant of the emperor stopped us at the door and called over his Gothic counterpart. To our surprise he led us to the Gothic side of the tent. We were shown to our seats, and as I sat down, I saw a familiar face staring back from the other side of the table.

It was Kniva.

We ate and drank too much, but it was still a fine evening.

At some point in time, Kniva, who was seated next to me, nudged me with his elbow. "Argunt is calling for you and Marcus to stand", he whispered.

I poked Marcus with my elbow and we stood, not knowing what to expect.

Argunt said some words and the Goths cheered us aloud, drinking to our good fortune.

I made to take my seat again, but Kniva stopped me by shaking his head imperceptibly. "You have to wait until the skald has finished his tale", he whispered. "It is a great honour bestowed on you by the iudex", he explained.

Marcus and I stood like idiots while the poet of the Goths sang our praises. The only benefit was that the Romans did not understand a word, although the emperor appraised us with an enquiring glance.

After what felt like eternity, we retook our seats. "It was a story about how you slew the giant Hygelac", he explained. "After you left, Argunt uncovered Hygelac's scheme of usurping his throne. He is grateful to us and he even singled me out as his adopted heir."

During the second watch of the following day, I was summoned to the Praetorium. Marcus was already waiting for me outside. He looked decidedly nervous.

He sighed. "Apparently the emperor speaks the Gothic tongue and he wants to discuss certain things with us."

We were ushered into the presence of the emperor by his bodyguards. Maximinus Thrax was in discussion with his son, both seated at a table.

Marcus and I came to attention.

Father and son finished their muted conversation. The emperor stood with his hands clenched behind his back, and I could see from the expression on his face that he was angry. Extremely angry.

"I am invited to a feast by the enemies of Rome. Guess who I find in the seats of honour of these enemies? My own men, whom I trust!" he growled.

His voice gained volume as he continued. "To add insult to injury, the poets of my enemies sing the praises of these so-called 'loyal soldiers'. They tell of victories in single combat. Things I know nothing about. Things that have not been mentioned in the official report."

His loud booming voice now took another step up and he yelled: "Do you take me for a fool? A stupid, big barbarian fool. Is that who you think I am?"

I had the wisdom to realise that any answer offered would have been the wrong one. Like Marcus, I focused my gaze on an imaginary spot somewhere in front of me, not daring to meet Maximinus's gaze.

From the corner of my eye I did notice his son slouch in his chair, having difficulty hiding his pleasure at his father's outrage and our discomfort.

Maximinus kicked at a chair. The unfortunate piece of furniture flew across the room and collapsed into pieces of kindling.

At that moment, Cornelius Carbo entered the tent. The Thracian turned to Carbo and said: "Take them away. They are to be executed in the morning."

Looking back I have often asked myself why, at that point, I did not kill everyone in the room, except Marcus, of course. It certainly crossed my mind. With ease I could have disarmed a bodyguard and used his weapon to slay the rest. The fact is I had not.

Part of me attributed it to the shock caused by our sudden reversal of fortune. But the version I decided on is that it was not the will of the gods.

Chapter 27 – Civilians (September 237 AD)

From the day of birth, death is a certainty. Any day could be the last day of one's life. This fact does generally not bother people.

It is strange how knowing the time and date of one's death changes this, especially when the time and date is the following morning.

Marcus and I were locked up in the same cell. A small, sturdy room with no windows, from which escape was impossible.

I learned that day that Marcus and I shared at least one character trait. No matter how gloomy the outlook, we were still not willing to give up hope.

Seeing that we were not in chains, we concocted a hare-brained scheme where we would disarm the guards and escape, using horses to swim across the Danube. Fortunately we never had to test our plan as Carbo visited us later that afternoon.

He threw us two unbleached tunics. "Put these on", he commanded.

We quickly changed and he continued: "As you know, the emperor holds Hostilius in high regard. They have fought together for years. He went to the emperor and begged for your lives. At first Maximinus refused, but then Hostilius told him how you had paid off Titinius to get rid of the rumour mongers."

"The Thracian is a hard man, but he understands that Hostilius's loyalty is paramount to his control over the legion. He agreed to pardon you, but as from this moment, you are discharged from the legion. You will leave with your lives intact, but your possessions will be divided amongst your century."

In silence, he led us to the gate of the fort. The legionaries on duty opened the gate on Carbo's command and he left us to walk away with only our tunics.

Just like that, in the blink of an eye, we were civilians again. We stopped fifty paces from the gate. We managed to get away with our lives, but we had lost our careers.

I could not help but recall Cai's unheeded advice. "Lucius, you must prepare for storm. Be careful not associate too closely with emperor." I felt like a fool. I had been forewarned, yet I ignored the advice.

We just stood there for a while, too flabbergasted to know what to do. Legionaries on the wall pointed their fingers at us and I could hear their laughter echoing off the walls.

"Marcus, we had better get away from here before the Thracian changes his mind", I said.

He nodded and we continued down the road towards the town of Noviodunum.

As we entered the gates of the town, a hooded figure fell in behind us. I heard the familiar voice of Pumilio. "Just keep walking, Umbra. Act as if I ain't here. Follow me when the time comes", he whispered.

He walked past us and when he was at least thirty paces ahead, he turned into a side alley.

We waited a while, loitering in the street and then followed him into the dark alley.

Pumilio pulled us into a doorway and related the story.

"Hostilius told us what had happened. The Thracian instructed him to divide your possessions amongst the century. All refused to take anything. It is a sure death curse to steal from Mars's favourite, it is. We all know that. So we decided somethin' different. All of us who owe you a life gave some coin. That meant all of us in the century. Hostilius and Optio Didius gave even more 'cause they owe you more than one life, see. We got you two fine horses, we did."

"Leave town and walk two miles down the Via Militaris on the way back to Sirmium. Turn off the road by the burnt-out wagon on the left and walk into the shrubs", he commanded.

He clasped each of our arms, turned to me and said: "It has been an honour serving with you, sir", and saluted.

As he turned around to leave, he added: "And be careful, the Thracian is a right bastard he is. He will send his guards to do his dirty work. I've heard them rumours too often."

Marcus and I did as Pumilio instructed. Next to the road we found Silentus holding the reins of two scruffy-looking horses with dilapidated saddles.

There were two bundles on the ground next to the horses. It was our personal possessions and weapons, smuggled out of the camp by my century. I was overcome with emotion. I had regained the jian sword and the Hunnic bow. Even the scale armour Bradakos had gifted me was there.

I embraced Silentus. "The lads from the first century all helped to smuggle these items from the fort. May Fortuna protect you, sir", he said.

I was shocked. Silentus actually spoke. He looked at me and said: "Of course I can speak, sir. I just don't fancy it."

We kept to the undergrowth on the side of the road, acutely aware of Pumilio's warning.

After a third of a watch, we decided that it would be better to put as much distance as possible between us and Maximinus Thrax. We led our horses to the road and mounted. I donned my scale armour and assisted Marcus to get into my chain mail.

Despite Pumilio's efforts, our mounts were not of the best quality. Both Marcus and I knew horses well and realised that we could travel no faster than a slow canter. In addition, we had to rest the horses frequently. It proved frustrating. Looking over our shoulders all the time, knowing that we had no chance to outrun the agents of the emperor should he wish to have us killed.

By the middle of the afternoon there was still no sign of pursuit, but I had a feeling, call it a premonition, that they were coming for us.

"Marcus, I know that these bastards are coming for us", I said. "It is just a feeling, but I have come to trust my feelings."

"It is common knowledge that the god of war speaks to you, my friend", Marcus replied. "I, for one, will not gainsay him."

I had been studying the surrounding area for a while and once I found a suitable spot, I called a halt. The sides of the road were inaccessible due to thick shrubs and loose rock – perfect for an ambush. In addition, it would allow Marcus and me a route of escape.

We spent a third of a watch preparing the ambush. Exhausted, we sat down on the side of the road to eat some of the stale bread Silentus added to our packs. We washed it down with the disgusting legionary issue wine which was watered down. In my mind's eye I could see Ursa taking huge gulps from my not-so-insignificant stash of high quality red wine. Of course, my century had failed to send any of it along.

I any event, we had just finished eating when we heard the unmistakeable sound of horsemen approaching.

The sound had an urgency to it as the riders were no doubt pushing their mounts to catch their elusive quarry.

I had chosen a flat area between two hills to act as the killing ground. The crests of the hill were about four hundred paces apart, with dense shrubbery on both sides of the rock-strewn ground. The horsemen would have no choice but to stay on the road.

Our horses were tethered just beyond the crest of the second hill. We were hidden in the cover provided by huge boulders on the side of the crest.

Twelve riders appeared. They were the Thracian and Germani bodyguards of the emperor. Big men, riding heavily muscled horses. Yet, in his haste, the emperor had made mistakes. There were only twelve of them and none carried bows, and to keep the weight to a minimum, they wore no armour. That was the second mistake.

I had given Marcus my Roxolani bow to use. He would start shooting when the enemy was within a hundred paces. Anything farther would just be a waste of arrows. My quiver contained forty arrows and Marcus had twenty at his disposal.

We would try to kill them all. To allow them to escape would only intensify the pursuit and enrage the emperor further. Their complete disappearance would be baffling, hopefully causing delay and confusion.

We allowed the horsemen to reach the midway point of the narrow valley. I had to show myself to enable me to shoot, and as I stepped out from behind the rocks, I released two arrows. The horsemen became aware of our presence when two of them dropped from their horses with broad-headed arrows embedded in their chests. I was used to shooting arrows from the back of a horse. Shooting with both feet firmly on the ground is like child's play in comparison.

My arrows were heavy hunting arrows, made to match the incredible power of the recurve Hunnic bow. Only eight riders reached the hundred paces mark when Marcus stepped out from behind cover, adding his arrows to the attack. We had agreed that he would aim for the horses rather than the riders, who presented a much smaller target.

As the riders were relatively close, I took aim with an almost flat trajectory and aimed for their heads. On impact, their heads were thrown back and they flew from the horses, dead before they hit the ground.

Marcus hit three of the horses which went to ground heavily, their riders crushed by the rolling mounts. Another hit the paved road with such force that his bones shattered.

The last rider died twenty paces away. For good measure I put two arrows in his chest as he was already waving his sword around dangerously. Better safe than sorry.

Dead men and horses littered the road.

It took time to gather the skittish horses that survived the attack. In the end, eight of the twelve remained uninjured. The rest were put out of their misery.

We needed coin so Marcus and I resorted to looting the dead. The guards of the emperor were well paid and most carried coin on their person, which was the barbarian way. We ended up with a substantial amount of gold and silver.

It took the rest of the afternoon and early evening to clean up the site of the massacre. We used our horses to drag the corpses of the guards and the dead horses off the road into the dense shrubs. The soil was hard. We had no tools so we heaped the corpses and piled rocks on top. That would keep the scavengers at bay for a while.

Although it was dark when we were done, we did not want to spend the night in the proximity of the dead. The men who were supposed to get rid of us actually did us a favour as both Marcus and I were now well dressed, having looted the best of the clothing of the guards.

We set our horses free and took the best of the saddles of the guards. Apart from the excellent horses we were riding, each of us had three spare mounts.

We camped well away from the road and did not light a fire. Marcus and I took turns to stand guard throughout the night, but it passed uneventfully.

Having woken up early, we re-arranged all our loot and armour on the spare horses, keeping only our bows and swords available in case of an emergency. We started off before first light, knowing that we would make excellent time back to Sirmium.

We rode like the wind, only stopping briefly to sleep, buy provisions, or change horses. Marcus and I wanted to reach our homes before the emperor could dispatch his cronies to confiscate our properties and possibly kill our loved ones.

No messenger could have kept up with us. We arrived at the outskirts of Sirmium within nine days. Two-thirds of a watch later we stood before the gate of my farm villa, utterly exhausted.

Cai opened the gate, with the Roxolani guards looking over his shoulder. "I expected you earlier. You must have dragged feet on way home." With that he turned on his heels and walked towards the living quarters.

I looked at Marcus and said: "He tends to be a bit of an oracle from time to time."

Both of us burst out laughing and followed Cai into our home while the guards secured the gate.

Segelinde had already formed a bond with Nik and Cai. That was clear to me. It actually made me feel slightly jealous. Nonetheless, I was glad to be re-united with her. Nik had been teaching her Latin and although she still struggled with forming the words, I could see that she understood a great deal of what was said when we conversed.

It was too late for Marcus to carry on to his farm, and he decided to spend the evening with us and share a meal.

Servants poured buckets of hot water into wooden tubs which were placed in our rooms. I was soaking in the hot water when Nik entered my room.

He sat down on my bed, a few paces away. "Segelinde is a wonderful woman", he said. "You have made a good choice."

"Nik, a lot has happened since my last visit", I replied. "I may have placed all of us in grave danger."

Nik nodded. "Cai told me about his dreams and visions. I knew some kind of trouble was upon us, but he speaks in riddles that is difficult to decipher."

"I just wanted to tell you about Segelinde", he said. "You can relay the rest of your story during dinner."

He rose slowly like the old man he was, and walked towards the door. "Before I forget, your friend Felix is doing a good job, and he fits right in. Cai has sent him into the hills with most of the horses, just in the event that there is trouble."

To call it dinner was an understatement. The cook had prepared roasted boar, wild fowl and even some fish caught in the small lake on the farm. Nik and Cai had tried their hand at making cheese and it was delicious. Needless to say, Nik produced some or other incredible red wine which he extorted from a wealthy farmer.

Marcus and I relayed the tale of the happenings since we had parted ways with Segelinde. The tale of my fight with Hygelac was told to Nik by Cai and Segelinde long before my arrival.

"We need to leave this place tomorrow morning at first light", Nik said. "Maximinus Thrax will send his dogs to kill all of us. His power is growing and he is a cruel bastard, or so I have heard."

Nik turned to Marcus. "You need to do the same", he said. "If you want to, you can join us. I know someone who will give us shelter."

Marcus nodded. "My father and mother have passed away long ago", he said. "My brothers run the family estate. I think it best that I travel with you, without even showing my face on their farm. I know them. They will not leave. Maybe the Thracian will leave them be."

"I am owed a favour by old Senator Crispinus", Nik said. "Let's just say that I assisted him to remove certain obstacles, if you know what I mean."

Of course, nobody knew what Nik meant, but we were all interested to know where we would be going.

"Crispinus is a favourite of the senate and he has an enormous villa in Aquileia", Nik explained.

We all looked confused, but Marcus was the one to pose the question. "Sir, where is Aquileia?"

Chapter 28 – Aquileia (October 237 AD)

We left the farm early. Our party consisted of Marcus and me, Cai, Nik, Segelinde, and three of the Roxolani who volunteered to travel with us.

The distance from Sirmium to Aquileia was just short of three hundred and fifty miles. The Huns could have made the trip in five days. We would be lucky if we made it in half a moon.

Nik was too old to travel fast. We would stop over in Siscia for a rest day, and later on in Emona for a day or two. Technically we were not fugitives, as we were pardoned by the emperor, but knowing Maximinus's vindictive nature, we looked over our shoulders continually.

Most of my gold was stashed away somewhere on the farm where no one would be able to find it, but I did bring enough to allow us to travel in comfort.

To reach Siscia took five days. Nik insisted that he was in good health, but I could see that the pace at which we travelled affected him.

We arrived at the gates of Siscia late one afternoon. I was not familiar with the town, but Nik led us to an upmarket inn. We were dressed like wealthy merchants and we rode quality horses. The guards at the gate admitted us without a second glance. Nik and Cai shared a room, as did Marcus and me. Segelinde had her own room, and the Roxolani shared.

The owner of the inn was a heavy-set man. It soon became evident that he revelled in exchanging gossip. It might even have been a sideline business.

We were served whole roast fowl, heavily spiced with garum. The meat was complemented by a light red wine which we enjoyed neat. Afterwards our host brought us platters of cheese and thinly sliced smoked pork, accompanied by a dark fruity red wine.

Our host sat with us as we enjoyed the platters and wine. I could see that he was itching to exchange gossip. "I heard that there are certain 'problems' in the province of Africa and the mob in Rome is on the verge of rioting", he said, testing the waters.

He was no fool, and he did not indicate where his loyalties lay.

He looked at us with eyes filled with expectation - to either choose sides or provide news from the east.

"What kind of problems?" Nik asked.

Again, our host replied without commitment. "I am only a simple innkeeper and politics is far above my understanding. I only repeat what I hear."

Nik decided to repay his information with some news. "We did hear that the emperor is on his way back to Sirmium after meeting with the barbarians at Noviodunum ad Istrum."

"My news is fresh. Real fresh", the innkeeper replied. "The emperor will probably only find out when he reaches Sirmium."

"Then you will probably soon see the army moving through Siscia en route to Rome, eh?" Nik said. "To crush any uprising and all." Nik was only toying with him, not knowing that his words were to be prophetic.

The man turned white in the face. "I just hope there is no trouble. Trouble is bad for business, you know. I will have to find out if the city prefect is a supporter of the emperor."

"Thank you for the advance warning, my friends", he said. He signalled to a servant to attend him and soon enough the man appeared with a small amphorae of wine.

"Something special for my guests for warning me about impending danger", he added.

He left as the excellent dessert wine was poured. No doubt trying to establish whether Ciscia, and his skin, were at risk.

We left early the following morning, heading for Aquileia via Emona.

September was not the ideal time to cross the Alps, but it was still accessible.

We made camp early every afternoon, piled a huge fire, and made sure that Nik was snug in his tent after a warm meal.

Most of us were used to the bitter cold of the Sea of Grass so to us the Alps were bearable.

The weather held during our passage across the passes. We descended along the heavily wooded slopes until we reached the fertile plain below.

We travelled through vineyards, olive groves and miles and miles of fruit orchards. Aquileia was truly blessed by the gods.

Nik rode up to me from behind and pointed to a stone villa perched against a low hill. "That red you like so much. It is made there. When we go home to the farm, we will take a wagon and make sure we fill up the cellar properly." He winked at me, knowing our shared love for red wine.

Later that same day, the walls of the city came into view above the fruit and olive trees. In times past, this border city must have been a formidable fortress. Thick stone walls towered thirty feet above the surrounding landscape. The city was built with the Natiso River bordering the eastern and southern walls. Stone bridges led to gates in the wall, providing access on both sides. As we neared the bridge over the river, I noticed that the walls were in a state of disrepair. In some instances the walls had completely collapsed. The residents did not view the wall as necessary for defence, but treated it like a relic from a bygone era. Since the borders of the Empire had expanded hundreds, if not thousands of miles in all directions, walls were of little significance.

The city was at peace and we walked through the open gates without a question. Nik knew his way and led us to the affluent part of the city.

We came to a halt in front of an enormous villa. It was a veritable fortress in its own right. Nik used the hilt of his sword to knock against the iron reinforced gates.

We waited a few heartbeats. The gate opened and two burly guards appeared with a heavy-set man in tow.

"What is your business at the house of Senator Crispinus?" he said.

Nik dismounted and replied: "Tell your master that the Olympian is here to see him."

The man had the typical look of someone on the verge of complaining or denying a request, but Nik, being a patrician, had a certain way about him which cannot be taught. Fortunately the servant recognized this immediately. "I will do as you request, sir", he replied.

We waited for a while until the man reappeared with his master in tow. The master was clearly too young to be the old senator that Nik referred to. He walked up to Nik. "I am Rutilius Pudens Crispinus, what is the purpose of your visit?" he asked.

Nik's eyes were cast downward. "Is your father still on this side of the Styx?"

"He has not been for many years, sir", Crispinus replied.

"Then I bid you farewell", Nik sighed, clearly saddened by the news.

As Nik turned around to leave, Crispinus said: "Did you say that the Olympian is here?"

"My close friends used to call me the Olympian", Nik said in reply.

Crispinus's eyes drifted over us. "Please, allow me to show you some hospitality while we talk."

The gates opened and our whole party was admitted. Servants led the horses away to the stables and Nik gestured to the Roxolani to remain behind to guard our possessions. The rest of us followed our host into the atrium. Crispinus whispered instructions to his servants and soon slaves appeared carrying trays of fruit juice blended with ice.

He turned towards Nik. "Please follow me", he said.

Nik placed his hand on my arm. "I request that my son joins us", Nik said.

Crispinus nodded and we followed him along a hallway to the study.

Like the rest of the villa, the study was spacious. Hundreds of pigeon holes filled with scrolls lined the walls. Crispinus gestured to couches. "Please take a seat."

He walked to a desk in the corner of the room and fumbled inside a drawer, eventually producing a small scroll. Crispinus held the scroll aloft. "The lawyer who held my father's will gave this to me after the reading. I had nearly forgotten about this, until today." He sat down on the couch opposite and proceeded to read the scroll aloud.

My Son

As you know by now, you are the sole beneficiary of my sizeable estate and many assets. You also know that there are no amounts owed to anyone, no debts at all.

However, that is not entirely the truth.

There is a single debt owed by me. It is not a monetary debt quantifiable in coin. The debt, however, is real and may be called in at any time. It is a debt of honour.

Allow me to explain.

Many years ago, before the year of your birth, our family stood on the edge of a precipice. Other powerful men were in the same predicament. None possessed the power to remedy the situation.

There was one man who had the means to set things right. And he did, at great cost to himself. He lost all. His family, his assets, and nearly his life.

To his friends, he is simply referred to as 'the Olympian'. Should he ever appear on your doorstep, repay the debt to restore the honour of our family. Provide him freely with all that he asks of you, even if it amounts to half our wealth. It is a small price to pay.

How will you know this man? You will know in your heart when he mentions his name. If you are still uncertain, you will notice that he always carries a bow in a leather case tied to the saddle of his horse.

Rutilius Pudens Crispinus the Elder

He rolled the scroll back up and placed it back in the drawer.

He sat down again. "I will not ask of you to explain to me how the debt originated", he said. "I am sure that if I knew the truth, it would just place me in some kind of danger. The only thing I ask is how I may repay this debt. What is it that you require?"

Nik cleared his throat. "My son and his friend were both officers of the Legio IV Italica", he said. "As you know, the fourth is stationed at Sirmium and forms part of the army of Pannonia."

At the mention of the army of Pannonia, I could see a ghost of a frown appearing on his face.

"They both fell out of favour with the emperor, Maximinus Thrax", Nik added. "Officially they were pardoned, but discharged from the legion. They still fear for their lives, as they have affronted the most powerful man in Rome. A man with very little capacity for forgiveness, as you know. We have left our farm in Sirmium under the care of the manager. We need sanctuary for a while. Maybe a month or three. We have coin and we will gladly pay our way."

Crispinus sighed a breath of relief. "You ask very little of me in repayment of such a large debt", he said. "You will stay with me here in Aquileia. You will not pay one obol, on that I insist and it is final. The servants will ready the guest wing for you and I will assign you a cook and the necessary help. Your horses and guards will be looked after. It is the least I can do."

Nik nodded his thanks. "There is one other thing I ask."

"Anything", Crispinus replied.

"I need a supply of the best red wine in Aquileia. You will know better than most, as you own farms and trade in wine."

Crispinus smiled for the first time. "I can see why you were friends with my father", he said. "Do not be concerned. I will personally select the wine that will be made available to you. Most are from my own farms."

Chapter 29 – Rest

It was awkward at best, initially at least, to live the life of a wealthy patrician. I had spent my time with the eastern nomads, followed by two years in the legions.

In Aquileia we lived in luxury, as guests in the home of the wealthiest man in the city. We enjoyed the best food and drank the best wine available in the Empire. The residence even had its own baths and a hypocaust system to keep the villa warm in the winter.

Segelinde and I decided to postpone our wedding until we were safely back on the farm. We spent every day in each other's company, visiting the races, the market and the forum. Her Latin was improving daily and I could at least follow the thread of the conversation when she spoke in her native tongue.

Marcus and I sparred every day after training in the gymnasium. We ran races in the vast vineyards surrounding the city to improve our fitness, and I practised my archery. Cai trained with me in private, his oath not allowing him to impart his skill to Marcus.

I dined with my friends and my father every evening, falling into a habit of enjoying a little too much red wine while talking late into the night. Life was good. And my uneasiness was growing by the day.

Every now and again Crispinus would invite us to dine with him. He lived alone in the house and I think that he actually enjoyed our company.

On a particular evening in early December, we were sipping another spicy, yet fruity red with a dark purple colour.

"I had news from Rome today", Crispinus said. "Trouble has been brewing in Africa for some time now, but it has taken an interesting turn. The Africans have proclaimed the old Senator Gordian as the new emperor. I don't know about that, eh? He has governed many provinces and he has a good track record, but he is older than eighty years. But most importantly, he has no army to back him. I am sure that the Thracian will crush this revolt and nothing will come of it."

Nik sipped on his wine. "I believe that it is a good idea to start repairing the walls of the city and improve the battlements?"

Crispinus frowned in reply to Nik's statement. "Aquileia is a peaceful city. We will not choose sides should there be strife between the senate and the emperor", he said.

"I will sketch a scenario - how I see this unfolding", Nik said. "Tension has been building ever since Thrax had been declared emperor. He hates Rome and the senate. They hate him. I have even heard rumours that the praetorian prefect, Vitalianus, is terrorising Rome in the name of the emperor."

Crispinus nodded in agreement. "Go on. I agree with all you have said."

"At some time in the future the strife between the emperor and the senate will boil over", Nik continued. "In all likelihood, Thrax will march on Rome to assert his authority. You do realise that Aquileia will be on his path?"

Crispinus nodded.

Nik drank deeply from the cup. "The senate would surely request that you oppose Thrax and withhold supplies from his legions. If that is the case, you would have a choice to either side with Thrax or with the senate. Should your walls be in disrepair, you would have no choice. You would have to welcome Thrax with open arms and trust that he emerges victorious. If he does not, the new emperor supported by the senate will take away all from the elders of this city in reprisal of their support of Thrax."

Crispinus did not reply. He drank from his cup until he had to refill it. After a long, uncomfortable silence, he said: "Your logic cannot be faulted. I will meet with the other senator of consular rank who resides in the city. Tullus Menophilus is an intelligent and streetwise man. I would hear his opinion."

Nearly a month passed until we would see Crispinus again. We spent our time enjoying life and improving our martial prowess.

On one particularly cold evening, early in January 238, our presence was requested in the study of Crispinus.

As was the norm, he handed us cups filled with some rare vintage of red wine.

Crispinus brought us up to date. "After you raised your concerns at our last get-together, I met with Menophilus the following day. We agreed on a course of action. Ever since that day, we have been transporting the necessary stone and building material into the building yards of the city. We have also been stockpiling food and firewood. We have done all this without creating panic or suspicion. We have cited the reason for the building material as a planned extension to the arena and stockpiling of the food as preparation for a feast and games. Only Menophilus and I know the real reason for our actions."

He was interrupted by a knock on the door. A servant appeared and said: "A messenger has arrived. I have provided him with refreshments in the atrium, sir."

Crispinus excused himself, closing the door behind him to afford us privacy.

"Cai keeps rambling on about the gathering storm", Nik said. "I tend to think that these are the first signs, but it may well be years before the storm erupts."

Of course, Nik was completely wrong. The storm was there already and we were about to find out.

Crispinus appeared moments later, his complexion ashen.

He looked at us in turn. "A messenger from the senate delivered this." He waved the scroll about. "Gordian the elder sent his quaestor from Africa to assassinate Thrax's henchman, Vitalianus, the praetorian prefect in Rome. Thereafter, anarchy erupted in Rome. Maximinus's supporters were killed on a grand scale and general anarchy reigns. The senate has ratified the appointment of old senator Gordian and his son as joint emperors." He held up the scroll. "This is a request from the senate to revolt against Thrax and support their actions. Every major city and province in the Empire have been sent such a letter. Maximinus Thrax will know of this in days, if he doesn't already."

Like every other evening our small party dined together. Nik and I shared the information with Cai, Segelinde and Marcus.

"Fortunate thing that Thrax too busy fighting with senate to chase after you and Marcus. He now has bigger fish to fry", Cai said.

He was right of course, but it did nothing to improve our predicament, or that of Aquileia.

Slowly, by way of messengers, gossip, informants as well as word of mouth, news of the happenings trickled into a generally nervous city.

Meanwhile labourers, slaves and volunteers feverishly worked side by side to repair the walls and build additional towers to better the defences. Marcus and I volunteered to labour for free and we worked from dawn to dusk. Many times we returned home with bleeding hands or a variety of cuts and bruises.

The next significant piece of news was that Maximinus Thrax had marched from Sirmium. He was gathering the legions stationed on the Danube, and congregating in Siscia, which had opened their gates and declared in support of Maximinus. He sent his Pannonian legions ahead to prepare the way for the main force.

It was early February when we received the news that the two Gordians had both been killed in Africa by one of the Thracian's loyal governors in charge of Numidia. The senate did not sit on their laurels, and immediately appointed two of their own as replacements. Balbinus and Papienus were appointed as joint emperors and as an added twist, the mob insisted that the young grandson of Gordian be elevated to the status of 'heir apparent' by being given the title 'Caesar'.

By late March, the repairs on the wall were finished and the additional towers completed.

It was at this time that Crispinus summoned Marcus and me. We were shown into the study where the senator was reading from a scroll. He immediately abandoned his reading and stood to welcome us.

"The people tell me that you have done well in assisting the Aquileians in repairing the wall. They say that you each did the work of three men." He leaned towards us and said in a conspiratorial tone: "It improves my standing with the populace, as they know that you are guests in my house."

He handed us both the customary cup of wine, took a swallow from his, and gestured for us to take a seat. "The elders of the town met this morning as a result of the happenings, which you are acutely aware of. We decided to obey the senate and defy Maximinus Thrax. It is a risky move for sure, but the die is cast. We have sent missives to the senate to confirm our decision."

I knew where this was heading. "Please tell me how we may be of assistance, sir", I said.

"Nik tells me that you are both accomplished soldiers, yes?" Crispinus asked.

"I have accompanied Thrax on his campaign into Germania and Scythia, so yes, I have seen some action", Marcus replied. "But I would like to warn you, sir, Lucius is as close as a man can get to being the god of war himself."

"I need capable men to show the civilians the basics of fighting", Crispinus explained. "Else there is no way we will be able to defend the wall. I suggest you accompany me to the circus, the racing arena. We will use that for the purpose of training our people."

"Do you have your own bow?" he asked.

"I do, sir", I replied, "but I am a bit rusty."

Crispinus wished to see our martial ability with his own eyes. I understood. The destiny of all in the city depended upon our success.

We arrived at the circus, where two guards flanked the entrance. The senator nodded and the guards parted to let us in.

Inside the arena, servants had set up stakes and straw targets. It was similar to the training area of a typical Roman legion.

"I am impressed", I said.

Crispinus smiled. "Thank you, Lucius", he said. "I used to be a tribune in the legions. Long ago."

He pointed to a straw target one hundred and fifty paces away. "Show me", he said.

I took my Hunnic bow from its leather case and strung it. He stared at the weapon with undisguised curiosity. "I have seen a Scythian bow, but this, I have never laid eyes on. Where did you come by such a weapon?"

"Sir, far to the east of the Scythians there are a people most skilful and ferocious. They are people of the horse and fight with a bow. I lived with them before I joined the legions."

Crispinus raised his eyebrows and held out his hand. I handed him the bow and he studied it.

"Traditionally, the bow is a favoured weapon of the Aquileians", he said.

It was my turn to raise my eyebrows. "That is good news", I replied. "It might just make the difference."

While we talked I retrieved my quiver and placed five arrows in my draw hand.

He pointed in the general direction of a target and I took the strung bow from him. In less than the same amount of heartbeats I hit the target five times, the arrows grouped within the space of a hand.

"Are you as good with a sword?" he asked.

"Much, much better", I replied.

As a result of my words, Marcus was not tested.

Chapter 30 – Master of weapons (February 238 AD)

Marcus was an excellent swordsman and a useful bowman, measured in terms of Roman standards.

What I was about to learn was that Marcus's organizing skills were far superior to mine.

It was early in the morning and thousands of men queued in front of the gates of the Circus.

During the last days, we had spent time with Crispinus and collected a motley bunch of army veterans who knew their business. These twenty selected men stood behind us in the arena. They had been briefed by Marcus.

The purpose of the veterans was to divide the men into three groups. The first group being skilled men, the second being men with some skill or commitment and the third group being the useless rabble.

Within six days we managed to assess more than fifty thousand men. We ended up with three thousand skilled men and twenty thousand committed men who had some skill. The rest were practically worthless.

Most of the skilled men possessed armour. Either from serving in the legions, or from a relative who served in the legions.

The committed men had some armour and most of the useless mob had none.

Marcus and I first spent three days refreshing the skills of the experienced men. We practised the basics - thrusting with a sword, throwing a pilum and shooting with a bow. Once we were happy with the skilled men, we assigned a thousand of those men to train the twenty thousand semi-skilled men.

The residual two thousand skilled men had the task of trying to teach the basics to the twenty thousand useless sods. Each were given ten 'students' to teach.

We employed some of the legionary basics like 'marching' around the city and practising with training swords against the posts.

I must confess that on the third day I was close to giving up when Marcus took me aside. "Lucius, nobody is as good as you are. Nobody. We will never turn these men into gods of war. The only thing we can do is to give them the best chance of survival against the men of the legions. Remember, they will not be facing the legionaries on equal terms. They will be behind thirty foot walls, while the enemy will be clambering up rickety ladders. All we can do is the best that we are able to do."

I realised that only a miracle could save us. So I did the logical thing and sat down to talk with the only man I knew who could work miracles.

Cai sat cross-legged on the woollen carpet. "Lucuis of the Da Qin, I cannot train men of city", he said. "You know I have taken oath?"

"I know that Cai, but I am in need of more than that anyway. I am in need of a miracle", I sighed.

Cai smiled slyly. "That good, Lucius of the Da Qin, I take no oaths to hinder me perform miracles."

Cai inhaled deeply, closed his eyes as if he tried to remember a time long gone. "In the year that you born, warlord Cao Cao of the Wei, attacked Hanzhong where we lived. Before attack, we made substance that assist us overcome attackers. We never use it, as Master received vision to the contrary."

Cai stood and walked over to a small chest standing on a table in the corner of his room. He placed a stack of pieces of parchment on the table and methodically scrutinized them. After a while of searching he held up a scrap of paper decorated with the outlandish writings of the east.

"I copy recipe before all went up in flames", he said, and sat down again.

"Lucius, this I need", he said, and proceeded to scribble on a scrap of parchment.

I was able to procure the necessary with relative ease and I delivered it to Cai within a watch.

Cai worked late into the night in the privacy of his own room. The next morning he demonstrated the effect.

Within an hour, we had assembled Crispinus, Marcus and Nik.

Cai ignited the mixture in a wooden bowl and poured some into a bucket of water. It burned fiercely and extremely hot, incinerating the bowl in no time. The liquid even kept on burning as it floated on the water in the bucket. While burning, the liquid emitted a dark yellow smoke that caused serious bouts of coughing, and burning eyes.

Crispinus looked on in silence. "This is a most terrible weapon, my friends."

"It thin and run easily, but once ignited, it impossible to extinguish", Cai explained.

"What do you require to manufacture more?" Crispinus asked.

"I need barrels of olive oil and pitch, great quantities of yellow stone you call brimstone, and couple of wagon loads fired lime", Cai answered. He handed a wax tablet to Crispinus with the quantities required.

Crispinus studied the tablet. "You are fortunate, olive oil is freely available and there is much lime left over from making concrete for the walls. We use brimstone ground down to a powder to clean our clay and wood vessels we store wine in. Many hundreds of barrels are stored within the city warehouses. The boat builders are sure to have pitch available. I will send for all that you need immediately. I will arrange that all be delivered to a warehouse close to the eastern wall. When they attack, that is where it will take place."

I think that Cai and Nik suddenly found a new hobby, and to my surprise, Segelinde decided to assist.

But that was not where it ended.

Segelinde explained to me one evening while we were talking over a mug of wine. "I am sure that we will be able to make enough of Cai's flaming liquid, but we need a method of delivery. Throwing it on the attacker with buckets will only cause us to unsettle the warriors on the wall. We need a delivery system."

I was impressed. The love of my life was becoming a killer. Must be the Gothic blood, I thought.

In any event, a couple of days later she showed me their answer to the problem, which was twofold. With the assistance of Crispinus they had manufactured hundreds of small metal pots, attached to spear shafts which were about ten feet long. The pots would be filled, ignited and then extended over the wall, and emptied. It was lightweight, and could be used by women and children without exposing themselves from behind the battlements on the wall.

What was more impressive was the small catapult that Cai had built. It could hurl a small amphora filled with the burning liquid up to three hundred paces.

"I make twenty of these little things. I call 'surprise from Serica'", Cai said with a grin.

At this time, news reached us of Maximinus's arrival at Emona on the other side of the Alps. He apparently found the town deserted and burnt beyond recognition. The townsfolk had scurried off into the woods and the hills, taking their treasure, food and livestock with them before burning it themselves. This obviously had deprived the Thracian of supplies, but he interpreted it as a sign of what was to come, expecting all the towns en route to flee in the face of his mighty army.

The builders of the wall had also not been idle. With the wall and towers done, a ditch was excavated on the outside of the eastern and northern walls. Stakes were hammered into the ditches and sharpened. To my surprise, the ditch filled with water within a day or two. Crispinus explained that it was thanks to the proximity of the river.

The men were as ready as they were going to be, given the short period available to us. That which they lacked in skill, they made up for in morale. We had thousands of spears, and tens of thousands of arrows stockpiled. The town's warehouses were filled with provisions. All of the many wells had been cleaned, and supplied more water than could be consumed.

A couple of thousand folk living in the neighbouring countryside fled to the town, boosting the numbers of defenders significantly. We possessed such an abundance of supplies that the extra mouths were no problem.

Chapter 31 – Pannonian legions (March 238 AD)

If Italia had an army at the ready, chances are they would have met Maximinus in the narrow passes of the Alps. But alas, as the Pannonian legions crossed the Alps, no opposing force interfered. The main reason being that Pupienus was still assembling such a force - a collection of veterans and new recruits from all over Italy.

The Pannonians ended up laughing their way down the slopes. They destroyed farms and cut down trees, leaving a desolate landscape in their wake. But their quest to gain supplies was ineffectual as all the supplies were either within Aquileia or long gone with the local populace.

Aquileia had closed its gates. We were as ready as could be.

On a Tuesday afternoon on the Ides of March, we sighted the vanguard of the Thracian's army - the mighty legions from Pannonia.

The two Pannonian legions crossed the river and constructed a marching camp on the northeastern side of the city. Although we were buffered by the city's mighty walls, a Roman legion is still something to behold. It is a mighty war machine clad in iron, designed to grind down the enemy until none is left to oppose it. Roman legions had conquered most of the known world.

At least there was one positive. In the back of my mind I dreaded coming face-to-face with my former comrades, and I experienced great relief when I did not notice the standard of my former legion.

When we had finished our evening meal, Segelinde called me aside and led me to her room. She gestured for me to take a seat on her bed. "Kniva gave me something that I am supposed to give to you as a wedding present. It is something that he gained from the treasure chest of Hygelac the White. He felt that it belonged to you because you defeated the giant Heruli."

She took a leather pouch from a chest and placed it on the bed beside her, removed the contents, and held it to the light. It was magnificent, shining like the sun in the light of the oil lamp.

"It is bronze scale armour", she said. "Every scale is covered with gold and inscribed with a battle rune. This armour was made to protect the wearer in battle. Each rune represents a spell, cast to keep the wearer safe. I would have you take it and wear it to keep you safe." Segelinde started to sob and I held her for long, until it subsided.

"Segelinde, I will wear this tomorrow and every day I am on the wall", I promised.

This seemed to satisfy her and she calmed. "It is good, Eochar", she said. "It gives me much comfort."

The next morning, the Pannonians busied themselves with the demolishment of the dwellings outside the walls of the city. They used the wood to construct scaling ladders. I could kick myself that I did not insist on putting these outbuildings to the torch. I guess men do learn from their mistakes.

By the third watch of the day, on a Wednesday, the army assembled in front of the walls. Ready for war.

A small contingent marched forward, led by a tribune. Initially I thought that it was a party interested in a parley, but we saw no peace branches or white flags.

The group came to a halt about sixty paces from the wall. The tribune proceeded to speak with a booming voice and it soon became evident that he had been chosen for the task based on the volume of his voice, rather than his intelligence.

"People of Aquileia, you have closed your gates to the army of Pannonia and you have turned your back on your emperor. We have come in peace to deal with the usurpers in Rome, but you chose to join the enemy...", and so on and so forth.

Nobody was really interested and we all knew that, should we open the gates, the army would sack the city and most of the people inside would die.

I don't remember half of his ramblings, but he eventually concluded with: "But if you repent, if you open the gates and hand over the ringleaders of the revolt, we will spare the city. Else, before the sun sets today, we will burn the town and everything in it will burn to ash."

His last words were ironic, because in that instant, Cai decided to test the range of his 'surprise from Serica', and the jar containing the brimstone mixture crashed to the ground three feet from the tribune, whose whole body burst into flames. We all watched the spectacle with amazement, and unsurprisingly, the Pannonians launched their attack.

The Pannonian legions, which I had been part of until my recent fall from grace, spent their time guarding the limes and sometimes had to defend against a barbarian invasion. From time to time they would venture inside enemy territory and launch a counterstrike in retaliation.

The one thing the legions, especially the Pannonians, had not done for a while, was to lay siege to a city.

The old saying of 'the more you do it, the easier it gets' also applies to the inverse. 'If you rarely do it, you will find it a challenge.' And that was precisely what happened to the attackers when they stormed the walls.

While we were preparing for the siege, Cai was adamant that we should refrain from employing all our tricks to repel the initial attack, but keep some surprises for later. We just had to do enough to ensure that there would be a 'later on'.

"To destroy the will, firstly, hope need be created. A belief that goal can be accomplished. Then, hope need be utterly crushed. None must remain. Despair soon occupies void left by hope that has departed", Cai said, and smiled wickedly. "Only then does will to fight wither and die."

It was a gamble, but we decided not to use the brimstone mixture during the initial attack. To increase our chances of survival, we however had another surprise in store.

For weeks the smiths had been making caltrops. Two three-inch pieces of U-shaped metal are welded together like a cross, and the four points sharpened. The caltrop's claim to fame is that no matter how they fall on the ground, one wicked spike always points upwards.

Thousands of these caltrops were spread on the ground, starting thirty paces from the walls.

It was overcast, with only a watch of daylight left. It provided an indication of the measure of the confidence of the Pannonians. They thought they would be inside the city before it was too dark to fight.

In any event, we waited patiently while they advanced on the wall. There was no mad rush. The legions always moved with measured inevitability, which made them even more intimidating.

When they were fifty paces away, they started a slow jog. The men carrying the ladders moved to the front, each shielded by a comrade carrying a shield. It was obvious that the ladders had a dual purpose. They would first lay them across the ditch and secondly use them to scale the walls.

Up to this point in time, all the defenders did was watch. We had our bows at the ready, but it would be a waste of precious arrows to shoot into the advancing soldiers, as almost all of them would end up embedded in the rectangular shields. They would most probably have used the testudo formation where the overlapping shields cover the battle units like a shell protects a tortoise.

As the enemy soldiers entered the area seeded with caltrops, it was however a different story. The ranks lost cohesion as men stumbled, dropping shields and ladders. At once, thousands of arrows descended into the broken front ranks of the attackers. Most of the archers had no aim to speak of, but it was not needed. They could not miss. Legionaries fell by the hundreds, but they kept coming.

As we had agreed beforehand, the storm of arrows tapered off until no more arrows fell within their ranks. This was to create the illusion that our supply of arrows were dwindling, or had run out.

The Pannonians gained confidence and soon hundreds of ladders were placed against the walls, with legionaries feverishly trying to reach the battlements.

We were well prepared. The men worked in groups of three. One would hold a shield and a spear while two would each wield a long shaft with a metal hook at the tip. This they would use to drag the ladders to the side. Coincidentally, drawing the ladders to the side is much more effectual, and easier than trying to push them backwards. To push a ladder backwards requires enormous strength, especially when the ladder is encumbered by armour-clad legionaries.

Again, thousands of legionaries were injured, or died, when the ladders fell over, in some cases even taking another ladder with it.

But inevitably some legionaries made it to the top of the rampart. The big danger was that they would gain a foothold on the wall which could lead to them taking the city. But we had devised a plan to deal with it. For lack of a better word, I will call it reserves.

We had twenty groups of reserves, each made up of ten men, with each group responsible for thirty paces of the wall. Our reserve was made up of myself, Cai, Marcus and seven other Aquileians who proved to be skilful with a spear or a blade.

As soon as we noticed a potential problem, we would move in to address it. In most cases it involved the rest of us looking on as Cai dispatched one snarling legionary after another without breaking a sweat.

Close to sunset, the commanders of the legion must have reluctantly realised that defeat was inevitable. Almost all the ladders were destroyed and the men had been unable to gain a foothold. We heard the buccina signal the retreat.

As the legionaries withdrew from the field, the setting sun appeared from behind the clouds with the rays catching the defenders on the wall.

Illuminated by the last rays of the sun, my golden armour and helmet shone with an unearthly glow. My Hunnic bow was inlaid with silver leaf, and even that reflected the sun. I must have resembled Apollo as the Romans fled the field. Realising what was happening, I capitalized and released a few arrows in quick succession, felling retreating legionaries close to three hundred paces from the wall. Many of the Romans pointed in my direction and soon almost the entire legion was staring at the wall as the sun disappeared behind the horizon.

We left sentries on the wall when we retired to our quarters that evening.

We knew the next attack would come soon.

No attack took place the following day. The Romans did send an envoy requesting a truce to enable them to deal with the dead in front of the wall. Crispinus agreed to the request, which allowed us to take stock of our own situation. We did not emerge from the attack unscathed. Close to eighty men had lost their lives. We used the time at our disposal to burn the corpses of the dead while we recited the necessary prayers. They would be remembered as heroes.

The Pannonian legions had lost at least seven hundred men, based on the count made by the sentries.

The second attack was initiated at dawn the following day. Like Cai predicted, they were convinced that they could take the city. Again, they had made hundreds of siege ladders. This time I noticed that the ladders had two stabilizing poles attached to the sides of the ladders. Two men would hold the poles to ensure that it could not be pushed backwards or drawn over.

Hundreds of men carried fagots on their backs - piles of brushwood tied together that would be used to fill the ditch in front of the wall. I believe that if they had known that we would use burning liquid as a defence, they would have passed up on the brushwood.

The men placing the fagots were well protected by their comrades and we realised that trying to deter them was a waste of arrows. Soon the enemy was at the base of the wall, the soldiers scaling the tall ladders held stable by their comrades.

We had prepared well for this moment, and hundreds of women and older children set to work. Each team of three had a barrel filled with Cai's brimstone mixture. They stood behind the men defending the wall, filled up their buckets and set the contents alight with torches. Each small bucket was attached to a ten feet shaft. They used this to pour the burning contents onto the defenders ascending the ladders, or the legionaries waiting in line. It was akin to a rain of fire and brimstone. None could defend against the abomination that left the legionaries horribly burned, maimed and scarred.

I was watching the spectacle in horror when the fagots used to fill the ditch also caught fire. The scene deteriorated into one of total carnage. Hundreds of legionaries would never fight again, even if they survived. I was ashamed to say that our plan had been successful.

The burning mixture had an additional sting in the tail. The soldiers who inhaled the terrible fumes either collapsed or had to be carried to safety.

Without a doubt, we had broken the will of the Pannonians.

We allowed them to remove their dead and wounded and afterwards they retreated to their camp. They did not attack the walls again.

Our sentries relayed another piece of information that they overheard as the legionaries gathered their dead from underneath the walls. Apparently the men had seen a vision of the god Belenus fighting with the Aquileians on the wall. They refused to launch another attack as they were convinced that they fought against a god, rather than the simple folk of the city. Some survivors swore that they had control of the rampart when Belenus appeared and summoned a strange slanted-eyed demon to vanquish them. They had made up their minds. Aquileia could not be taken if the gods had decided otherwise.

That evening Crispinus dined with us. The city was exceptionally well provisioned and his cooks did not hold back. We were served lamb prepared with eastern spices and dates. Our host had laid on a selection of white and red wine paired with different cheeses from Gaul.

After dinner, while sipping red wine, I relayed the story told to me by the sentries, to our host and my friends.

At first, a slight smile appeared on Crispinus's face, and then faded again. I thought that I had offended him in some way, but Cai summarised it well. "Enemy might just have provided you with weapon to defeat them."

Crispinus and Nik exchanged a knowing glance. Then the senator excused himself and said: "Forgive me, friends, I have much work to do tonight."

Chapter 32 – The emperor arrives (April/May 238 AD)

It took the emperor half a moon to arrive at the walls of Aquileia.

We had broken the will of the Pannonians, but the actions of Maximinus Thrax crushed whatever remained. When he was told of the repeated failed attacks on the city, the emperor executed the legates and head tribunes of the two Pannonian legions on account of cowardice.

Soon after, the first official emissary arrived. Thrax had chosen a man who hailed from the city and whose family was still within the walls. The tribune stood before the walls, accompanied by several centurions.

He spoke under a branch of truce and therefore he would not be harmed. He relayed a message from the emperor that if the gates were to be opened, the people of the city would be pardoned. The officer made it clear that 'others' were the guilty ones and not them. Everyone knowing that 'others' meant anyone in the city who possessed significant wealth. Wealth that could bolster the coffers of the emperor.

The tribune continued, explaining how the emperor would be merciful towards the city should they do the right thing. It was strangely amusing because, of the many things Maximinus was, merciful was certainly not one of them.

The people listened silently from the walls, obviously considering the man's words carefully as their lives depended on making the right choice.

Once the tribune was done, Crispinus provided his views in a speech from the wall. He was well-loved by the people of the city and had won their trust over the years. And he possessed a weapon which was infinitely more powerful than anything a mortal man could lay his hands on. He wielded it then with considerable skill.

"The patron god of Aquileia, our beloved Belenus, has shown his support for the city as he descended from the heavens and fought by our side. How else could the mighty legions of Rome be defeated? Even the enemy had seen the vision of Belenus appearing on the walls. The men of the Pannonian legions can testify to it being the truth. They had been defeated not by men, but by the gods themselves. Not foreign gods, but the gods of Rome. Would you choose to defy the gods?"

Well, who could offer a reply to that?

The tribune skulked away while the oracles proclaimed the certain victory of the city.

In retrospect, Maximinus Thrax made one fatal mistake. He was an experienced soldier and should have anticipated that the desperation of the Pannonian legions would infect the rest of the army.

Within days exaggerated rumours of gods and demons had spread throughout the whole of the army. Who would choose to defy the will of the gods and condemn their shades to eternal torment?

Although half of the city's walls were bordered by a river, the emperor chose to encircle the entire city.

His problems were not confined to the animosity of the gods. He had expected to be supplied by the Italian cities as he advanced on Rome. Now the first major city had closed its gates. The army was low on provisions after crossing the Alps and they needed the stores of Aquileia desperately. Already the troops survived on half rations, and the water in the river was fouled by the dead.

When it became clear that the city would not yield, the army began to construct siege towers. In addition, they initiated tunnels that would see the walls undermined and destroyed.

While the army prepared, augurs and oracles shouted the prophesied victory of the Aquileians from the walls. The army became increasingly desperate. The confidence of the city soared.

Crispinus stood next to me while I watched the undermining activity with increased concern. He took me by the arm and led me away from the walls. Close by was one of the many wells that the city used for its fresh water supply. As he neared, the people made way and allowed us to approach. We looked into the well and then he led me back to the battlements.

The water level in the well was less than three feet from the surface. Crispinus pointed to the activity of the hundreds of legionaries busy with the undermining. "Many of them will drown in the tunnels as they near the walls. The water lies close to the surface. They are wasting their time."

The siege towers were completed the following day. They were constructed three hundred paces from the wall, just outside of the perceived arrow range.

I walked over to Cai, who was studying the enemy from one of the towers on the battlements. He was taking aim with a fire catapult.

"Why not destroy them now?" I asked.

"It requires enormous effort to drag towers close to walls. When fifty paces from wall, then I burn them", he said, smiling. "Make them work for no benefit, will help break will of army."

And so it happened - thousands laboured for hours to drag the terrible siege towers closer to the walls. The siege towers should have been covered by raw cow hides to protect them from fire, but as there were no cows available, they remained uncovered.

When the engines stood fifty paces from the walls, Cai and his helpers simply moved from one catapult to another and unleashed his deadly brimstone mixture on the towers. The legionaries carried ample supplies of water to counter such attempts to fire the structures, but Cai's fires could not be extinguished with water and before long the towers were reduced to ash.

The undermining went on day and night, and the enemy must have been close to the walls when hundreds of men spilled out of the entry points of the mines, yelling and shouting in despair. They had encountered the water veins of Aquileia, and the mines flooded and collapsed.

On the walls, the priests of Belenus gave thanks to their god for delivering them from the unjustly attack by the invaders. The people of the city cheered.

It continued for another month. Attack after attack. Eventually the reluctance of the soldiers became visible. Most just going through the motions, believing that they were doomed to fail.

The army was close to starvation, the soldiers demoralised and infected with dysentery from drinking the fouled water. Crispinus had long before denied the army access to their dead. Consequently, dead and rotting corpses littered the battlefield. Soldiers who refused to attack the walls were publicly executed. The Thracian was losing control of his legions.

While we were fighting for our lives, elsewhere in Italy Pupienus and the senate were labouring as well. Harbours were evacuated of ships, roads and passes were walled, and the army of the Thracian was cut off from the rest of the world. Rumours spread that Pupienus had assembled the largest army in the history of Rome, made up of veterans and recruits. They were marching on Aquileia and were set on destroying the starving army of Maximinus Thrax. In addition, they had taken the women and children who lived on the Alban Mountain close to Rome, as hostages. To clarify, these were the women and children of the men of the Legio II Parthica. It was all nonsense, of course, but the besieging army had no way of knowing it.

But yet, I believe one action of the emperor broke the proverbial back of the camel. The Thracian announced that he had decided to name his son "Caesar", which meant that he would be the heir apparent. It was a significant mistake.

The soldiers secretly despised the pretty boy son of the emperor who afforded no respect to the men of the legions. He encouraged the men from the safety of horseback, sending thousands to their death without ever fighting himself.

One afternoon early in May, the besiegers were beaten back once again and the Thracian had no choice but to have his men retire for the day. As the attack had started early in the morning, the legions were given leave for the day to lick their wounds.

Allow me to digress.

Traditionally, the Praetorian Guard was the personal army and protectors of the emperor. During his reign, forty years earlier, Septimius Severus increased the numbers of the Praetorians to ten thousand men. In addition, he based the Legio II Parthica twelve miles outside of Rome in a fortress on the Alban Mountain. Unsurprisingly they were known as the Albanians. By doing this, he had created a combat ready force of fifteen thousand veteran troops who acted as a reserve in case their assistance was required by the emperor.

The Praetorian threat had been neutralised by the earlier assassination of their prefect and by the ongoing battles between them and the mob in Rome. The new prefect supported the boy, Gordian III, therefore the Guard was not available to assist Maximinus Thrax.

The Albanians acted like a mobile Praetorian Guard and had been travelling with the Thracian ever since they assisted with the assassination of the previous emperor. They were also the ones who had elevated Maximinus to emperor.

In any event, many rumours were circulating, hence the Albanians became increasingly concerned about the safety of their relatives on the Alban Mountain. Apparently they sent the standard bearer, Felsonius Verus, to secretly speak with the disgruntled head centurions of the legions. The Primi Pili, fed up with the Thracian, wielded the true power and they agreed to support the Albanians if they rose against the emperor.

On that fateful afternoon Felsonius Verus ripped the insignia of Maximinus Thrax from the standard of the Legio II Parthica and paraded it through the camp of the legions.

A mob of representatives of the aggrieved Albanians marched to the emperor's tent with murder on their minds. The guards, who were also Albanians, turned a blind eye. Tempers flared, resulting in the assassination of the Thracian and his arrogant son.

Fearing retribution by the legates and friends of the Thracian, the lead centurions of the other legions rose in simultaneous revolt and assassinated them all.

Chapter 33 – Deliverance

The fighting had been severe during the morning and we all retired to the home of our host. I enjoyed a hot bath to wash the dust and gore from my tired body.

The servants had prepared a light meal and I took a cup of white wine with it.

The combination of the wine and food coupled with the bath made me retire to my room early, and I fell into a deep dreamless sleep.

Two watches passed in the blink of an eye.

Marcus woke me. "Lucius, you had better come quickly. There is a commotion in the Roman camp. They might be preparing for an all-out attack."

I groggily donned my armour and soon after followed Marcus to join the rest of our party on the battlements.

Crispinus and Menophilus stood close to us as we witnessed thousands of men from the army advance towards the wall. I readied myself mentally to repel yet another attack, but as the men came closer I realised that they wore no armour, nor did they carry any weapons. They were led by a party of officers who still wore their official garb and armour. I soon realised that they were the Primi Pili of the legions of the besieging army. All the standard bearers were there, carrying the golden eagle standards of all the legions present.

A man stepped forward. "I am Aurelius Dizza, Primus Pilus of the II Parthica. The emperor, Maximinus Thrax, has been killed for his defiance of the senate of Rome", he boomed.

Silence reigned for at least sixty heartbeats.

Crispinus then answered: "The new emperors of the Empire have been chosen by the senate and the people." He continued and named the chosen two senators and the younger boy Gordian, who was heir apparent. When he was done, the people on the walls of Aquileia started to cheer and shout the names of the new emperors.

The thousands of soldiers in front of the wall stood watching in silence.

Crispinus lifted his hands for silence, and as the cheering died down he asked the soldiers: "Does the mighty army of the Rhine and the Danube not honour their emperors, legitimately chosen by the senate and the people of Rome?"

It started with a single cheer, then another, and soon the soldiers were cheering the names of the new emperors, the people of the city joining in from the walls.

"Would it be wise to open the gates of the city to them?" I asked Crispinus.

He smiled, waved at the crowd. "I agree with you, Lucius, the soldiers are too fickle. They might decide to proclaim one of their own as emperor again. Like they did with the Thracian. It might also be that this is a ruse by Maximinus himself."

Soon a body of horsemen appeared and the soldiers made way for them. They rode up to the walls, displaying the heads of Maximinus and his son on spear shafts.

"Well, at least it is no ruse of the Thracian", he said, "but I will refuse to open the gates until one of the new emperors arrive with an army at his back."

I nodded in agreement. "We do need to give these soldiers access to supplies. They are close to starvation. I suggest that we set up a small market outside the gates and sell them what they require." I thought for a moment and added: "Without inflating the prices."

Crispinus replied to the leader of the soldiers: "Primus Pilus Dizza. I will allow you to clear away the dead from around these walls and I will provide you with enough free wine and meat to toast your fallen comrades on their way to Elysium. At the second watch of tomorrow morning, you can purchase all you need at a market we will set up outside the walls. The wine will be delivered by wagon to the camp within a third of a watch."

The soldiers acknowledged his words with an almighty cheer.

The next morning vendors set up stalls just outside the main gate of Aquileia. They sold bread, grain, olive oil, meat and all kinds of food that could be imagined. In addition, there were stalls selling wine - from the most basic to the best vintages available in the Empire. They also sold cloaks, blankets and boots.

After the sun had set, the soldiers were still purchasing goods to satisfy their basic needs. At the request of the traders of the city, Crispinus had torches carried outside so that the trading could continue deep into the night.

It went on for many days, and settled into a routine where the traders would set up their stalls outside the walls for half of the day. The soldiers were well fed and had more than enough wine available to keep themselves at the desired level of inebriation. To summarise, the soldiers were content.

In less than two weeks Pupienus arrived with an army at his back. The army kept well away from the city and I imagine the reason for the secrecy was its diminutive size, although it is impossible to be certain.

Pupienus forgave the men of the legions and they kissed and made up - the II Parthica returning to the Albian Mountains and the other legions returning to the frontiers where they were stationed.

The new emperor resided as a guest in the home of our host, Crispinus. Once he had taken care of business, he stayed on for a couple of days at the house of his friend.

One evening our group was invited to dine with the emperor as well as our host.

We expected it to be a stiff affair, but I would imagine it would not have been unlike dining with Crispinus and his father. Pupienus was a genial old senator who got on especially well with Nik and Cai.

At one stage during the evening, the emperor said: "Crispinus, you and the people of Aquileia are the saviours of the whole of Italy. If you had opened the gates to the Thracian, I do not think that Rome could have resisted him."

"We really have the god Belenus to thank for our salvation, my friend", Crispinus said.

Pupienus frowned, not knowing where the conversation was heading, but our host continued with a smile: "I will explain." He told the story of how my presence on the wall inspired the belief that the god was fighting against the Pannonian legions in person. He also gave credit to Cai for brewing the potent brimstone mixture.

My respect for Crispinus increased tenfold, as he was not afraid to share the glory.

The emperor turned to Marcus and me and said: "How may I repay you for what you have done for Rome?"

Marcus and I had discussed this beforehand and he replied: "There is one thing. Lucius and I were both officers in the Legio IV Italica until we had a fallout with the Thracian. Two officers placed their lives on the line to save us. Cornelius Carbo, the lead tribune, and Primus Pilus Hostilius Proculus. They are good soldiers, and loyal to Rome. They have remained in Sirmium to command the cohorts that remained to guard the limes."

Pupienus looked at Marcus and replied: "What you ask is not advancement for yourself, but pardon for your comrades."

He sighed, and drank deeply from his cup. "When you look at me, what you see is an old man. I was a Primus Pilus in the army of Caracalla many years ago. I served as an imperial legate and while I governed Germania, our armies emerged victorious against the Alemanni and the Yazyges. In my heart, I will always be a man of the legions."

He turned the cup in his hand. "What you ask is no small thing, but what you have achieved in Aquileia outweighs it."

He turned to Crispinus. "Arrange for the newly appointed imperial legate and governor of Pannonia Inferior to report to me tomorrow before they depart for Sirmium."

"I make no oaths, but I will discuss it with my people and even provide new written orders if it is required", Pupienus added.

On the insistence of Crispinus we remained in the city for another ten days. It felt like a holiday after the almost continuous fighting during the preceding months. I spent most of my time in the company of Segelinde. We grew closer, only confirming that we had made the right decision.

Ten days later we excited the city via the western gate and took the road leading north, heading back the way we came months before.

Our party travelled at a snail's pace, blaming it on the two wagons fully loaded with some of the best red wine available in Italy. Apart from providing us with this gift, he committed to sending us two wagon loads of the same every year. Crispinus justified it by reasoning that by providing us with sanctuary we had eventually helped him more than he had helped us and that he was honour bound to reward us. He told us that he would be richly rewarded by Pupienus and Gordian, and that he felt obliged to pass some of the benefits on to us. We did not argue with his solid reasoning. In addition, we had made a friend for life.

In the end it took the best part of a moon to travel back to my farm near Sirmium. Marcus accompanied us to the farm and I insisted that three of our barbarian guards escort him home. It turned out to be a good decision. They were attacked by a group of seven brigands, whose scalps now decorate the saddles of my Scythians' horses.

Chapter 34 – Family heritage

Apart from planning our wedding, we had a more secretive agenda to attend to. That was the reason my future bride and I travelled to Sirmium.

I had discussed my plans at length with Segelinde, who was in agreement. For now, I decided to keep it as a surprise for Nik and Cai.

As was the norm, the area around the procurator's office was reasonably crowded with people standing in line to meet with officials who shared the same building.

I did not have an appointment with Alexander, the secretary to the procurator, but I was unconcerned. Underneath my cloak I carried a purse heavy with gold.

It only cost me one silver coin to be ushered into the presence of the clerk. He had someone in attendance, although unfortunately for him, he was immediately dismissed.

Alexander motioned for us to be seated. He inclined his head to me. "I can see that you are getting on in the world, Lucius Domitius. Who is this beautiful lady?"

I interrupted him before he could continue to flatter Segelinde, who had a reasonable command of Latin by then.

"My dear Alexander, it is exactly the reason why I have come to visit with you. I need you to introduce this Roman lady to me", I replied.

Alexander sat with a confused expression. He raised his eyebrows and nodded slowly, as understanding dawned on him. "Well, well, well. I am certainly able to introduce you to her, but I require some information."

He took his stylus in his hand and started scribbling on a wax tablet.

"Is she of equestrian or common birth?"

"She is of noble birth, Alexander. I would think from the line of Emperor Traianus. But distant family will be acceptable."

"Was she born in Pannonia Inferior or maybe somewhere else?" the Greek asked.

"I would think Dacia, but anywhere close will do. Maybe Moesia or even Dalmatia", I replied.

He looked up from his notes and smiled. "These things are not cheap, you know."

"I would certainly not expect them to be cheap, but I need them to be watertight", I said.

I placed the purse with fifty gold coins on the table. He took it without opening it or counting the coins, only testing the weight before securing it to his belt underneath his tunic.

"Gold", I said.

He nodded and replied: "I would expect nothing less."

"I assume the documents legalizing our marriage are covered by the fee?" I asked.

He nodded, now all business. "It's all part of the service, Lucius."

He stood and excused himself. "I may be away for some time. I will send a slave with decent wine. It's also included in the fee", he said and winked before he left.

It took a long time. I guess he was away for the most part of a watch.

When he returned, the little Greek appeared physically exhausted. He was sweating and wiped his brow with the back of his hand.

"This was most challenging, most challenging", he muttered to himself as he placed some scrolls on the table.

Before he continued, he summoned a slave and ordered more iced wine.

He suddenly smiled. "My dear Lucius Domitius Aurelianus, it is my pleasure to introduce you to Ulpia Severina, daughter of Ulpius Crinitus. She is a descendant from the line of Traianus and was born in Dacia."

Before I had time to interrupt, he handed me a scroll. "This is the official marriage document. Congratulations, you make a fine couple."

I clasped his arm and retook my seat. "May I see the scroll you are looking at?"

He handed it to me, I studied it, and handed it back.

"Of course that will have to be destroyed and copied from afresh", he explained.

I nodded and bid him farewell.

That is the tale of how a Gothic princess became a Roman lady, a descendant from the imperial line of Traianus.

Chapter 35 – Visitor

I handed the marriage document to Nik. He stared at it for a while, a broad smile slowly forming on his face. He turned to Segelinde. "I am proud to have you as my daughter-in-law, Ulpia Severina."

He clasped my arm. "You are showing me that you may have potential", he said with a grin.

He slapped me on the back and left the room, his laughter echoing down the hallway.

Cai and Felix appeared heartbeats later. They had both taken a liking to Segelinde.

"Umbra, Nik told us you have the papers", Felix said. "Now you have to give the girl a wedding to remember. I will stand for nothing less." Cai stood beside him, nodding his head in agreement. Both had obviously gone over to Segelinde's side.

In a typical Roman wedding, the bride wove her own dress. Also, there was supposed to be a procession from the house of the bride to the house of the groom. The problem was that we did not have separate homes, neither did we have enough guests for the dinner party.

Segelinde and I decided to do the best with what we had. She told me without blushing that she wished to have a dress made.

"It is a Gothic tradition", she explained, although I had my doubts.

We visited Sirmium and at the stalls of the dressmakers we ordered a magnificent embroidered dress.

I had nearly no family and Segelinde's family was a thousand miles away. We had no alternative but to keep it small. Still, we arranged for a musician, juggler and dancers to provide entertainment at the feast. I thought about inviting my old comrades in the legion, but legionaries are not granted random leave, so I discarded the idea. As Marcus was a civilian as well, he was invited.

Segelinde chose a date that was auspicious for weddings according to her culture, and we made all the arrangements. I even arranged for a cook and his team from Sirmium to assist our servants with the preparation of the food for the feast.

My bride was insistent on adhering to my culture as far as possible. On the evening preceding the wedding, Segelinde donned her ordered dress and a flame-yellow veil made of silk, compliments of Cai. Felix lit a torch dedicated to the goddess Ceres and led her and Cai, who acted as her father, in a procession around our villa, symbolising the bride's journey to the husband's house.

Nik and I met her at the gate, where she gave Nik a copper coin as a sign that she would be living in her husband's home from then on. Nik, also carrying a torch, handed it, as well as a small bowl of water to Cai, who accepted it on behalf of Segelinde.

"I give you fire and water", Nik said.

Felix handed his torch to Nik and carried Segelinde over the threshold of the gate.

She said to me: "I am where you are." I repeated her words and we clasped right hands.

Officially we were married.

I led her to the bedroom.

We slept late the next morning, enjoying each other's company. We eventually emerged and found that a delicious, but light, breakfast awaited us. We ate slowly, savouring our private time together.

Nik had arranged baths to be prepared, and my bride and I retired to our own rooms to ready ourselves for the festivities.

I had just begun to doze off when there was an urgent knock on the door. A moment later Cai walked in. "A visitor has arrived", he said.

"Just show Marcus to the spare room. He would understand", I replied.

"Marcus arrived two-thirds of watch ago", Cai said. "He enjoying bath in spare room. This is other visitor. Come see now."

I quickly dried and slipped into a clean tunic, following a shuffling Cai to the atrium.

Hostilius was dressed in full military garb. He was drinking wine from a cup held in his right hand, while his left hand was held behind his back, holding his helmet.

Without thinking, I came to attention. "It is good to see you, sir."

He waved away the formality and clasped my arm, following me into the study.

We sat down on couches while a servant brought a jug of wine and two additional cups.

Within moments Marcus walked in. The former tribune smiled broadly and nodded to the Primus Pilus.

He sat down next to me, both of us facing Hostilius.

Hostilius told his story.

"The Thracian left the IV Italica behind when he marched off to Rome. We sent cohort-sized vexillations to guard all the fortresses abandoned by the legions he took with him on campaign. Carbo told me that the emperor left us behind because he needed people he could depend on to look after things while he was away. I think he left us behind because we fell out of favour with him after the whole incident concerning you and Marcus. It's all guesswork. Not that it matters anymore."

He drank deeply from his cup and continued. "I was left here at Sirmium. We started hearing rumours that things weren't going smoothly with the campaign. Strange tales about the gods fighting against the legions of Pannonia." He studied me with a gaze filled with suspicion, and took another swallow.

"Then a detachment from the Albanian legion arrived with an imperial order to place Carbo and me under arrest. We were locked up for three weeks. Three bloody weeks! We heard that the emperor was assassinated and that we would most likely be executed."

"On the day of the execution we were frogmarched from the cells, but instead of losing our lives we were led to the Praetorium were the imperial legate was waiting for us. He had a scroll with him. We had been pardoned by the emperor himself. I saw the scroll, as well as the emperor's personal seal."

"I was reinstated as Primus Pilus, but Carbo was given a forced retirement with full honours."

"It is a good tale to hear, centurion", Marcus said. "Lucius and I toast to your good fortune." He raised his glass for a toast.

"Good fortune my arse", Hostilius replied, scowling.

"Let me tell you what I think really happened."

"When the Pannonian legions returned, they told stories of Belenus fighting on the side of the Aquileians. A god wielding a silver bow. Like the one you have, incidentally. They said that at times he summoned a small slanted-eyed demon from the underworld to do his killing for him."

"Sound familiar yet?"

"But what really gave it away was the other scroll the imperial legate had with him."

Hostilius was smiling now, with Marcus and I shifting around on the couch like guilty children.

"I think that you two somehow ended up in Aquileia and helped the townsfolk. And when Maximinus arrived, you gave his arse a proper kicking."

"That is truly a far-fetched tale, Centurion", I replied.

"Yes it is, isn't it", he said, still smiling, and produced a small scroll from a leather pouch, prominently displaying the intricate personal seal of the Roman Emperor.

Author's Note

I trust that you have enjoyed the second book in the series.

In many instances written history relating to this period has either been lost in the fog of time or it might never have been recorded. That is especially applicable to most of the tribes which Rome referred to as barbarians. These peoples did not record history by writing it down. They only appear in the written histories of the Greeks, Romans and Chinese, who often regarded them as enemies.

In any event, my aim is to be as historically accurate as possible, but I am sure that I inadvertently miss the target from time to time, in which case I apologise to the purists among my readers.

Kindly take the time to provide a rating and/or a review.

The Thrice Named Man, Part III, Sasanian, will be available soon.

www.HectorMillerBooks.com

Made in the USA
San Bernardino, CA
01 December 2019